THE
SECRET
CIRCLE

The Hunt

The Vampire Diaries novels

The Stefan's Diaries novels

The Secret Circle novels

Created by

L. J. SMITH

Written by Aubrey Clark

THE
SECRET
CIRCLE

The Hunt

HARPER TEEN

An Imprint of HarperCollinsPublishers

HarperTeen is an imprint of HarperCollins Publishers.

The Secret Circle: The Hunt

alloyentertainment
Produced by Alloy Entertainment
151 West 26th Street, New York, NY 10001
www.alloyentertainment.com

Library of Congress Cataloging-in-Publication Data is available.
ISBN 978-0-06-213042-6

Typography by Liz Dresner
12   13   14   15   16   CG/RRDH   10 9 8 7 6 5 4 3 2 1
❖
First Edition

THE
SECRET
CIRCLE

The Hunt

CHAPTER 1

Cassie held her father's Book of Shadows in her hands and shivered. There would be no going back, her mother had said, but now she watched Cassie expectantly.

The book's gold deckle-edged pages were cinched closed with a leather string, like a soft, thin belt. Cassie pulled on it, and dust particles flew into the air as its knot came undone, but the book's cover remained in place.

"It's not too late to change your mind," her mother said. "Are you sure you're ready?"

Cassie nodded. If this book contained the secrets to defeating her half sister, Scarlett, and saving the Circle from the hunters, it wasn't even a question. It was her duty to study it.

She carefully fanned open the book. Its spine cracked and Cassie's eyes seemed to meld to the page. The text scrawled upon the paper's yellowed surface was composed of squiggly lines and archaic symbols. The curl of each brushstroke felt forbidden, like Cassie had revealed something not intended for her eyes.

But before Cassie could process exactly what she was seeing, the book grew warm in her hands, and then threateningly hot. Within seconds the skin of her fingers was sizzling, and Cassie couldn't stop herself from crying out. Her flesh adhered to the book, and she couldn't pull her hands away despite the scorching pain.

Her mother's face was stricken with fear, but she acted fast. She raised her palm and with one wide swoop batted the book out of Cassie's hands and onto the floor.

Cassie released a whimper of relief, but the damage had been done. Her hands were singed red with throbbing, bubbling burns.

She looked at her mother, terrified. "You said it was just a book."

"It was. Or I thought it was." Her mother examined Cassie's injuries to see how serious they were. Then she glanced at where the book had landed facedown on the wooden floor. She moved toward it cautiously, picked it up without harm, and secured it closed by tightly retying the string.

"I'll put this somewhere safe for now," she said. "I'm sorry, Cassie. I had no idea that would happen. I've never seen anything like it."

"I don't understand." Cassie gaped at her mother, dizzy for answers. "You said I'd need this book to defeat Scarlett, but how can I study it if I can't even hold it?"

Her mother shook her head. "I don't know. It must be spelled, to keep it from being opened by anyone other than its owner."

"Then I have to figure out how to break the spell. Scarlett is out there somewhere, and she wants to kill me. That book is my only hope against her."

Her mother raised her hand to halt Cassie's anxious stream of consciousness. "One thing at a time. Our first priority is to tend to those burns. I think you've had enough excitement for one night."

She gave Cassie's shoulder a quick, loving squeeze, and then she ushered the book out of sight.

When she returned with an armful of gauze and ointment, Cassie's mind was racing with new questions and concern for her friends who'd been marked by the hunters. "Faye's and Laurel's lives might depend on me opening that book," Cassie said. "I have to try again."

Her mother sat beside her looking forlorn. "Faye and Laurel are in grave danger." She reached for Cassie's hands and began dressing the wounds. "But there are two steps to the process of witch hunters killing a witch: They catch you doing magic and you're marked, and only then can they perform the killing curse. If we can stop the hunters from performing the second step, your friends will be okay."

The killing curse. Cassie remembered the hunter mark, the aftermath of the curse on Melanie's aunt Constance's forehead the day she died. The Circle hadn't even known the hunters had marked her until it was too late.

"Why don't the hunters just perform the killing curse immediately after marking someone?" Cassie asked. "Why wait?"

"Because it takes just one hunter to mark someone, but the killing curse requires several of them." Cassie's mother wrapped the burns quickly and efficiently, like a battle-field nurse. "It's a process, much like a spell, so it can't just happen at any moment."

Cassie winced as the harsh gauze touched her raw skin.

"So Faye and Laurel will need to be protected," her mother said. "But tonight, the only thing for you to do is rest."

Cassie nodded. She still had so many questions, but the pain was making her weary. She moved to the comfort of her own bed and felt her eyes grow heavy. She allowed them to close as sleep overtook her. But even in the soft dark of her own eyelids, Cassie could see the glowing outline of her father's book shining against the black.

The next morning, Cassie's mind was still running in circles while she waited on her front porch for Adam to pick her up for school. She tried to relax, to admire the sun glinting red off the windows of each house on the bluff, but there was too much to be anxious about. In the past week Cassie had learned that her half sister wanted to kill her and take over the Circle—and she'd nearly succeeded. They'd had a confrontation in Cape Cod, and Cassie had chased Scarlett away, but she'd escaped with the Master Tools.

As if that weren't enough, there was also the issue of the hunters. The Circle was now sure that Max and his father—Principal Boylan—were witch hunters. They'd already marked Laurel and Faye with the hunter symbol, and it was possible they knew the identities of all the Circle members.

Cassie looked down at the gray paint peeling off the front porch. *This old house*, she thought, *this antiquated town*. There was no escaping its ancient history.

It was a sunny, windless day, but how could Cassie enjoy it? She pulled the sleeves of her purple hoodie down over her hands to cover her burns. She would have disappeared entirely into its soft cotton if she could. And then she heard something—a rustling in the bushes. *It's just the breeze*, she told herself, but not a single blade of grass stirred.

There was the crunching of leaves. It was coming from her left, along the row of shrubs that lined the path to the house's side door—an opportune place for an intruder to break in, or for Scarlett to sneak her way into Cassie's home.

Treading lightly across the rickety wooden porch, Cassie stepped closer to the sound. The shrubs moved again—this time she saw it with her own eyes—and she screamed, "Scarlett!"

An orange tabby cat shot out from the wavering hedge, zipping past Cassie and up a neighbor's tree. The cat's prey was left behind in the uncut grass: a sorry-looking field mouse. Cassie exhaled. She would have laughed out loud at herself if she weren't so embarrassed.

She walked back around to the front porch just as Adam pulled up to the curb. Her heart hadn't yet returned to its regular rhythm when she climbed into the passenger seat of his old Mustang and leaned over for a kiss.

"What were you doing in the backyard?" Adam asked as he pulled out of her driveway and onto Crowhaven Road. "Running laps? You're all sweaty."

"Is that any way to greet your girlfriend?" Cassie joked. "By telling her she's perspiring?"

Adam smiled. "I'm just saying you look hot, that's all. Hot and humid." He waited for her to laugh, and when she didn't he tilted his head at her apologetically.

Cassie appreciated Adam's sense of humor, even when he was teasing her. No matter how dire the situation was with the hunters and with Scarlett, Adam was still able to make light of things. Cassie needed that now more than ever.

She focused on the sparkle in his blue-gray eyes and thought of the silver cord, that mystifying bond that connected Adam's soul to hers. What did it mean that she'd also seen a cord connecting Adam to Scarlett on the night of their battle? Could she have imagined it? Cassie could hardly think about it. She reached for Adam's free hand and interlaced her fingers with his.

"Is that from the fire in Cape Cod?" Adam asked. He lifted Cassie's sleeve up, revealing the blistering spots on her left hand. "I didn't realize how bad these were before. Are they getting worse?"

Cassie remained silent, unsure of how to explain these new marks on her body, but her silence only misled Adam to believe he'd been correct about their source.

"We have to find Scarlett," he said. "She has to pay for this and everything else she's done." Cassie still didn't know what to say; the situation was much more complicated than that.

"How can you sit there so calmly?" He took his eyes off the road to momentarily glance at Cassie. "You've been physically, and most likely permanently, scarred by her. We can't let her get away with this."

"These burns aren't from my battle with Scarlett," Cassie said, more abruptly than she'd meant to. "They're from last night."

Adam slowed the car almost to a stop. "Last night? What happened last night?"

Cassie watched a crowded school bus zip past them on the left. Behind them, a frustrated tailgater honked his horn. "I don't want to keep any secrets from you," she said. "But if I tell you something, I need it to stay between us."

Adam pulled over to the side of the road and cut the engine, sensing this would require his full attention. "I think it goes without saying by this point, but you can trust me."

They were stopped in front of Sprinkles Donut Shop, and the air smelled like sugar and frosting.

"My mother gave me something last night. Something that had been hidden in my grandmother's house for a long time," Cassie said, and then paused. She knew she could tell Adam anything and he wouldn't judge her, but it was still difficult getting the words out.

"Don't tell me there are more Master Tools we didn't know about. That would be incredible." Adam's voice was hopeful in a way that made Cassie's heart break.

"No. But it is something that belonged to Black John."

Adam's posture straightened at the sound of Black John's name and he sat icily still.

"I have his Book of Shadows," Cassie said.

She watched Adam's expression turn from apprehensive to excited. "Are you serious?" he shouted. "Do you realize how much we can learn from that book?"

"There's more," Cassie said, before Adam could get carried away. "When I opened it, it was like the book turned against me, like it was alive in my hands. Just like when the Master Tools backfired on me when I was battling Scarlett."

Adam nodded, remembering how the Tools had obeyed Scarlett's black magic. They'd singed Cassie's skin just before they unhinged themselves from her body and flew at Scarlett's outstretched hands. "That explains the burns," he said. "But what's the connection between the two?"

"I think the book is spelled," Cassie said. "Something to prevent the wrong people from getting a hold of it. But it wasn't like I could read it anyway. It's written in some ancient language I've never seen before. It doesn't even look like words."

"We should have Diana search her Book of Shadows for information." Adam immediately went into strategizing mode. "There must be a way to break the book's spell. And we can all start researching the language. There's a chance it could be Sumerian, or even cuneiform. Black John's ancestors would go back that far."

"Adam," Cassie interrupted him. "Remember you agreed we could keep this between us?"

Adam's face dropped. He looked away momentarily. "But that was before I knew what it was."

"I'm sorry," Cassie said. "But I need to understand more of what this is before involving the rest of the Circle. This is about me and my father."

"It's a pretty big deal." Adam's voice hit that pitch it always did when he was exasperated. "We have to tell the Circle eventually."

"I know," Cassie said as gently as she could. She reminded herself that Adam's passion and perseverance were her favorite things about him. "I just need a little time."

She fiddled with the few strands of reddish-brown hair that had fallen in front of his eyes. "For now, let this be our secret."

Adam nodded, realizing he was pushing too hard. "Okay. But in the meantime I want to help in any way I can. I'll do research, whatever you need. Just name it."

Cassie felt her shoulders settle. "Thank you," she said, reaching out to him. "For now, all I need is your support."

"Always." Adam brought Cassie's injured hand to his warm lips and kissed it.

"I also need a chocolate glazed donut from Sprinkles," Cassie added.

"Your wish is my command." Adam leaned in, met Cassie's lips with his own, and kissed her without restraint. It felt good, and it felt right. Maybe there was hope for this day yet.

CHAPTER 2

Cassie was sitting in third-period history debating between (a) the Continental Congress and (b) the House of Representatives on her pop quiz, when a hall monitor came to the door and handed Ms. Darby a pink slip of paper.

"Laurel," Ms. Darby said. "Mr. Boylan wants to see you in his office right away."

Cassie's head shot up. She couldn't allow Laurel to be alone with the principal. He was a witch hunter, and Laurel had been marked.

Laurel looked at Cassie and then back at Ms. Darby. "But I haven't finished my test yet."

"You can make it up after school," Ms. Darby said. "The principal wouldn't call you out of class unless it was important."

Laurel hesitated.

"Go on." Ms. Darby pointed to the doorway. "If you're in trouble for something, standing here and keeping him waiting surely won't help matters any."

"Yes, ma'am," Laurel said.

Cassie watched her fearfully gather her books. What could she do to stop her?

Laurel handed her exam in to Ms. Darby and obediently followed the monitor out the door, glancing over her shoulder at Cassie one last time.

There were no other Circle members in class, so it was up to Cassie to do something. One way or another, she had to get herself into the principal's office. Laurel's life could be at stake.

Cassie quickly scribbled in the remaining empty blanks on her exam, and then rushed up to the front of the room.

"I'm done, Ms. Darby." She held her side and bit her lip. "And I'm not feeling so well. May I go to the nurse?"

Ms. Darby eyed Cassie, trying to discern if she was faking.

Cassie swallowed hard, cleared her throat, and leaned forward like she might puke right on Ms. Darby's desk.

"Go," Ms. Darby said, and Cassie bolted for the hallway.

She ran the whole way, ignoring multiple commands from teachers telling her to slow down, and arrived at the principal's office panting. Immediately, she could feel an energy in the air—something dark and morose. The door to Mr. Boylan's office was closed.

"Hi there, Cassie. What can I do for you?" asked Mrs. Karol, the perpetually rosy-cheeked office secretary.

"There's an emergency," Cassie said, catching Mrs. Karol by surprise. "In the gymnasium. A fight or something, I'm not sure, but people were screaming for someone to get the principal right away."

"Not again." Mrs. Karol scooted off her seat and hurried over to the principal's door. She knocked on it anxiously while turning the knob to let herself in.

"Sorry to interrupt," she said, "but I think we've got a brawl on our hands, down in the gymnasium."

Mr. Boylan jerked backward, away from Laurel, the moment the door opened. He patted down his salt-and-pepper hair and straightened his gray suit. "I'm a little busy here."

He backpedaled to his desk and grabbed a pen and

manila folder, presumably to appear more official. "And how many times have I told you, you can't just barge into my office like that."

"Don't you snap at me," Mrs. Karol said, with her bright smile fully intact. "It's not my fault your students behave like wild animals." She entered the room and took him by the elbow of his finely tailored jacket. "Now hurry up. You're the only one who can handle this."

Cassie spotted Laurel seated across from Mr. Boylan's large oak desk. She waved at her to try to catch her attention, but Laurel was entirely oblivious to everything going on around her. She was as pale as a ghost, and her eyes were focused on an invisible spot in front of her.

With a huff, Mr. Boylan followed Mrs. Karol toward the gymnasium. "Let's make this quick," he said, and then noticed Cassie for the first time.

"I won't be long," he called out to Laurel, while focusing directly on Cassie. "We'll pick up right where we left off when I return. You can count on it."

It sounded like a threat aimed at them both. Cassie shuddered at the thought of what she might have walked in on if she'd arrived only a few minutes later.

Laurel still hadn't moved a muscle, even after the principal and Mrs. Karol were out of sight. Cassie ran to her and shook her by her thin, delicate shoulders. "Are you all right? What did he do to you?"

Laurel's face slowly came back to life, and she finally noticed Cassie standing there. "We have to get out of here," she said, and leapt from her seat to run for the door.

Cassie grabbed her by the hand and led her down the hall to the science wing. "Steer clear of the gymnasium," she said, as she maneuvered Laurel in the opposite direction. It was only a matter of time before Mr. Boylan realized there wasn't any fight. "We need a place to hide. At least until the bell rings."

Down the wing, there was an unlocked supply closet. Cassie guided Laurel inside and closed the door behind them.

"It smells like formaldehyde in here," Laurel said.

Cassie didn't have the heart to alert Laurel, an avid animal lover, to the jarred pig fetus directly behind her. "You're right, it does," was all Cassie said, and then pulled Laurel in for a hug. "I'm just glad you're okay."

Among countless shelves of glass beakers and safety goggles, Laurel let herself cry and explained how Mr. Boylan had been interrogating her, trying to find out information about her friends.

"He was asking me about everyone in the Circle by

name," Laurel said. "And he was asking about our families. He knows we're all witches, Cassie, and he wants to mark every one of us."

Cassie was gradually putting the pieces together. "Then we absolutely can't perform magic until we figure out how to stop him."

Laurel's eyes welled up with tears again.

"You're okay now," Cassie assured her. "And you're not alone. We're going to figure out a way to save you. I promise."

"How? We are in over our heads, Cassie. This isn't like anything we've ever faced before." Laurel started to cry so furiously Cassie was afraid someone in the hallway would hear them. "I don't want to die," she said.

"*Shh.* Nobody is going to die." Cassie lowered her own voice to a whisper. "I've been talking to my mom about my father. Just last night in fact. And I'm learning things, Laurel. Ancient things that will help us."

Laurel's sobbing quieted and she wiped the tears from her rosy cheeks. "Really?" she asked.

"Really. When my father was young he saved a friend of my mother's who had been marked. I know it can be done."

"And you think you can figure out how he did it?"

"I know I can," Cassie said. She said everything she could think of to try to help Laurel calm down, but in her mind she feared they were running out of time. She had to do something about this—and her father's book—before the hunters picked them off one by one.

CHAPTER 3

Pink and white banners advertising the spring dance hung on all four walls of the school cafeteria. On a different day, or maybe in a different life, Cassie would have been excited for the dance. But this afternoon's lunch was going to be all business. Suzan arrived a few minutes after the others and dropped her tray on the table with enthusiasm, seemingly oblivious to the group's mood. "Is it that time already? We have to go shopping before all the good dresses disappear."

"Is that seriously what's on your mind right now?" Melanie said, her mouth half full. "A stupid dance?"

Suzan crossed her arms over her cerulean blouse. "We're supposed to act normal, right? So we don't seem suspicious to the principal or anyone else. I'm just acting normal."

"You can act however you want, as long as you don't perform any magic," Cassie announced. "The principal knows who we are. We confirmed that this morning."

Suzan took a seat between Faye and Deborah. "Oh." She pushed her tray away dejectedly. "Nobody told me. I'm always the last to know everything."

Cassie looked around the table at her friends. Of course the hunters had figured them out. Not only were they always together, but none of them seemed average, even when they were alone. Adam and Nick, the Henderson brothers, and even Sean carried themselves with a pride and independence that set them apart from other guys at school. Their fellow students were terrified and awe-struck by them. It was no different for the girls. Diana was the most admired, and Faye the most feared—but Laurel, Melanie, Deborah, and Suzan were no less intriguing to their classmates. Something about them sparkled. They were unlike all the other girls in school; their problems were so much larger than boys and clothes. It was stupid of Cassie to assume any of them could have remained unrecognized by the hunters.

"After what happened earlier today," Diana said quietly, "school is no longer safe for those of us who've been marked." She'd directed the comment at Laurel, but Laurel just played with her sandwich, not eating and not looking up. Cassie had never seen her this depressed, even when the hunters first burned their symbol onto her front lawn.

Faye also pretended not to hear Diana's warning. She refused to acknowledge that she'd been marked at all. Cassie noticed she was still wearing the opal necklace Max had given her, the one he'd stamped with the hunter symbol.

"You can take that off," Cassie said, pointing to the necklace. "You don't have to keep wearing it like some kind of scarlet letter."

Faye shook her head. "I'm not about to let on that I know about the mark. He's not the only one who can pretend to be someone he's not."

Deborah nodded, pointing her plastic fork at Faye like a spear. "You should give him a taste of his own medicine. Max played you, and now you have to turn it around on him."

"There he is." Sean shifted his beady eyes across the cafeteria toward Max, and Faye quickly applied a fresh coat of red gloss to her lips.

"Do you honestly think revenge is the best idea right now?" Diana asked. "We've already had one close call with a hunter today. We don't need another."

"Relax, D." Faye curled her lips into a smile. "We need information on the hunters and he's our way to it. I'm going to pump him for intel, double agent–style. Watch and learn."

Without another word, Faye stood up and jogged over to Max, meeting him halfway as he approached. He was dressed to go to lacrosse practice and carried a duffel bag. Faye took the bag from him, dropped it to her side, and pretended to be just as in love with him as ever. She pulled him in close and kissed him passionately on the mouth. "I've missed you," she said, loud enough for the Circle to hear.

Max touched his fingers to his lips, now lightly coated in the same red gloss as Faye's. "And I missed you," he said.

Max was tall and muscular with light brown hair. His voice was rugged, and he wore a perpetual cocky grin. He was just the kind of guy that made Faye swoon. It's no wonder she'd let her guard down enough to get marked by him.

The rest of the Circle watched as Faye whispered into Max's ear and he murmured back to her in a soft voice.

"Do you think he's falling for it?" Sean asked.

"Seems like it," Doug said, nodding his wild head of blond hair. "He's acting the same as before. Like a lovesick wimp."

"But who knows if she'll be able to get any information out of him," his twin brother said.

Melanie was dubious, as usual. "There's no way he's going to give up anything on the hunters. Whether he thinks Faye's on to him or not, he's not stupid."

"But Faye might be able to trick him into leading us to more of them," Nick said. He was sitting on the cafeteria table, bent over with his feet on a chair. "There have to be more hunters in town than just Max and his dad."

Melanie rolled her gray eyes. "Yeah, I'm sure Max will be happy to introduce us to all his hunter buddies. Maybe he'll even host a cocktail party."

Cassie continued watching Max and Faye's back-and-forth. It was almost comical, both of them pretending to be into the other when they were actually sworn enemies. But Max's face betrayed nothing more than he intended it to. He was running this show and Cassie could see he was too good at it to crack under a little pressure.

After a few minutes of the charade, Faye finally gave up. She leaned in and kissed Max one last time before returning to the group. Max waved as he passed them on his way to the gym, flashing his perfect smile—but Cassie thought it looked like he was grinning at Diana in particular.

"Well, that was a bust," Faye said. "He's either a really good actor or he doesn't know anything about what happened earlier in the principal's office. I mentioned my friend Laurel and he asked which one she was."

"We still shouldn't push our luck," Diana said. "I think it's time for you to distance yourself from him and his dad."

"I think Diana's right," Cassie said. "We need to lay down some new rules."

"Just what this Circle needs." Faye returned to her seat at the table. "More rules."

"What do you propose?" Diana asked, speaking over Faye. "We're listening."

Cassie realized she had the whole group's attention. They watched her hopefully, like she might have some secret panacea to solve all their problems. She cleared her throat and tried to think of something fast.

"Well, we know the hunters can't mark someone without witnessing them doing magic. But once they're marked, the next step is the killing curse, which means death. Ultimate death."

"Is this supposed to be a pep talk?" Sean called out.

"Let her finish." Nick glared at Sean with a deep mahogany stare.

"I think we need to enact a buddy system. One hunter can't perform the killing curse on a witch alone. The best thing we can do is make sure we're not alone either," Cassie said.

Deborah let out a whoop of laughter. "That's your big idea? For us to hold hands in the hallway like pre-schoolers?"

"I never said it was a big idea," Cassie said defensively. "It just makes sense for those of us who are marked to be with another Circle member at all times. Including overnight."

Faye's honey-colored eyes blazed. "No way. I won't agree to having a babysitter. I'd rather die."

"You just might die if you *don't* agree to this," Melanie said. "It's the only way we can be sure you and Laurel remain safe."

Laurel looked up from her untouched lunch. She

didn't appear any more eager than Faye to accept this new rule. "But Cassie, you said before that you've been talking to your mom about your father, and that you're learning ancient things that could help us."

Cassie felt herself tense up. She could sense Adam's cavernous eyes watching her, and she swore she could actually hear Diana's jaw unhinge before any words escaped her mouth.

"What ancient things?" Diana asked, with a hint of suspicion in her voice.

The entire cafeteria seemed to fall silent and Cassie shifted uncomfortably. "I was just telling Laurel that my father once saved someone who was marked. I'm trying to learn more about how he did it."

Diana furrowed her brow at Cassie's discomfort. She was unwilling to let the matter drop. "Do you think he used something similar to the witch-hunter curse we memorized from my Book of Shadows?"

"Probably something like that," Cassie said, trying to sound nonchalant and upbeat.

"Why don't we just use the witch-hunter curse from Diana's book now? We know Max and his dad are hunters," Suzan said. "I don't understand what we're waiting for."

"I second that," Nick said.

Diana released a frustrated breath. They'd been over this before. "Because this is our chance to use the hunters' ignorance for more information. We still have surprise on our side. They don't know we know who they are. And we also don't know for sure how that curse works, or what it'll do. It's a very rough translation, so it's our absolute last resort. If we try it and it doesn't work, then we'll all be marked in a matter of seconds."

"In other words," Faye said, "we have no clue if those words we memorized are a witch-hunter curse or a fairy tale."

Diana was quiet for a few seconds. She chewed on her lip nervously.

"We can't rely on that mediocre, pieced-together translation from Diana's book," Adam said. "No offense to you, Diana, but whatever curse Black John used, that's the one we want when we go up against the hunters."

Diana nodded and looked down at her hands. Adam turned to Cassie. She could tell he was struggling to restrain himself from telling the group about Black John's book, but she also knew he'd never betray her trust, no matter how difficult it was for him.

"What about the protection spell?" Laurel asked.

"Shouldn't that keep me and Faye safe enough so we can at least continue leading normal lives?"

"It seems to be intact." Diana raised her head, hesitantly. "But we don't know how long it'll last. That spell is kind of a one-shot deal, and once it wears off, that's it."

"And," Melanie said, "even if it does last, we can't be sure it's strong enough against the hunter's killing curse. It probably isn't."

Faye stared off into space, for once too upset to argue.

Cassie momentarily considered her own situation. If the protection spell wore off, she'd really be powerless against Scarlett. As it was, she was jumping at every shadow and freezing up at the sight of every redhead who walked by.

"How are you going to do it?" Faye called out to Cassie, like she'd just snapped out of a daydream. "How do you plan to figure out the curse Black John used?"

Cassie glanced at Adam, but his expression kept her secret safely hidden.

"I'm trying to learn what I can from my mother," Cassie said. "She's blocked out a lot of the past, but when I get her talking sometimes things come to light."

It was a good answer for being put on the spot, and even true. But Cassie knew it would take more to save her friends and defeat the hunters than simply getting her mother to talk about the past. She had to get her father's book back.

CHAPTER 4

Cassie's mother appeared at the top of the stairs the moment Cassie stepped through the door. "Good, it's you," she said. "I'm glad you're home."

"Were you expecting somebody else?"

"No need for sarcasm." Her mother descended the stairs. "I've been concerned about you since last night. Since the incident."

"Incident," Cassie said, as she dropped her bag on the kitchen table. "That's one way of putting it."

Her mother followed her into the kitchen. "Lift up your sleeves. Let me see your hands."

"They don't even hurt anymore," Cassie said, lying.

She pulled her sleeves back to reveal the aching burns. "They'll probably be gone in a few days."

But her mother persisted and carefully examined the marks. "I prepared an ointment for you from some herbs in the garden. It's cooling in the fridge."

Cassie sighed at her mother's safeguarding, but the truth was, she was grateful. She'd felt strange since she'd woken up that morning, and her burns had been throbbing all day.

Her mother fetched the stone mortar and pestle full of ointment from the fridge and took a seat at the kitchen table across from Cassie.

The ointment was pea green and smelled like skunk. Her mother mixed it with her fingers and reached for Cassie's hand. "The way that book heated up on you— I've never seen anything like it," she said. "I can't stop thinking about it."

She focused on applying the medicine gently and evenly. "I want you to be honest with me and tell me if you feel any other effects from what happened."

"Effects like wincing every time I opened one of my schoolbooks today?"

Her mother frowned. "This is serious, Cassie. I don't want you going near it again, at least not until we figure out how to disable the guarding spell. It's too dangerous."

Getting the book back from her mother was going to be more of a challenge than Cassie had anticipated. "But how else are we supposed to learn how to break the spell?" she asked. "It's not like there's anyone around here to ask."

Her mother was quiet for a few seconds. "Times like these, I wish your grandmother were still here. She knew a lot more about these things than I do."

Cassie had been thinking the same thing but hadn't had the heart to say it aloud. When her grandmother died, she took all her years of knowledge and wisdom with her. She was irreplaceable.

"At least I have you," Cassie said, and she meant it. She and her mother had come a long way over the past few months, and Cassie believed she could tell her almost anything.

As her mother wrapped Cassie's medicine-covered skin in fresh gauze, Cassie explained everything that had happened that morning with the principal. She didn't leave out a single detail; she was hoping to convince her mother how necessary it was to give the book another try.

"I wish there was some way we could keep Faye and

Laurel safe," she said. "Actually, that reminds me. Is there anything else you can remember about Black John saving your friend from the hunters when you were younger?"

Her mother thought for a moment. "It was some kind of spell. A curse, actually. I imagine it would be in his Book of Shadows."

The book. Cassie knew her question would lead right back to it.

"I remember your father once saying," her mother continued, "that the hunters themselves don't have power. They don't have magic. But they carry stone relics that have been passed down for centuries, and the relics are incredibly powerful. If the bond between hunter and relic can be broken, so can the marks on witches."

Cassie's eyes lit up—there was a way! But her mother paused and her voice took on a serious tone. "Now, Cassie, I know what you're thinking. You want to find that curse to save your friends, but you have to believe me when I tell you that you can't use magic from a book you don't understand. No dark magic can be used without grave consequences. Those burns on your hands were just the beginning."

Cassie agreed for the sake of her mother's peace of mind.

"But until we can figure out a way to use the book safely," her mother said, "I think I have another way to help. I know the perfect place to keep Faye and Laurel safe."

This was a turn Cassie hadn't anticipated. "Where?"

"Right here. There's a secret room in the house."

Cassie looked at her mother in disbelief. "You've got to be kidding me."

Her mother laughed. "Your grandmother built it when tensions between the townspeople and witches started rising sixteen years ago, just before the storm that claimed so many lives." She paused solemnly. "So many of your friends' parents' lives. She had it spelled for special protection. Come on, I'll show it to you."

Cassie followed her mother to the stairs that led to the basement. "Why didn't you tell me about this sooner?" she asked.

"You didn't need it then." Her mother led Cassie through the shadowy basement, which smelled of mold and mildew, and stopped in front of an old bookcase. "But you do now."

She raised her arms and rested her hands upon one of the dusty shelves. "I'm a little rusty," her mother said. "But I think I can do it." She closed her eyes and then focused her energy on the wall of books. She recited a wary chant in a tone of voice Cassie had never heard from her before:

Enchanted threshold—
door untold—
reveal to me what you conceal.

The edges of the bookshelf gradually began to glow, like the sun had just broken through a wall of clouds, and then a doorway appeared. Cassie couldn't believe her eyes. It was an enchanted opening—a rippling portal made visible in the center of the shelves, just large enough to step through.

Cassie's mother was pleased with her success. "I guess after all these years I've still got it," she said. "Go on, step inside."

Cassie cautiously crossed the threshold to look around. It was a large room, fully furnished like a studio apartment. There was a cast-iron bed, handmade lamps, and a tufted sofa. It was all so old-fashioned it looked antique, giving the space an unexpected elegance, like a nineteenth-century sitting room.

"It needs a good dusting, that's for sure," her mother

said. "But it'll do the job. Should I start preparing it for your friends?"

Cassie nodded. The room had its own kitchen nook and bathroom, and in the living room area there was even an old television set. "It's perfect," Cassie said. "Thank you."

They wasted no time getting started. Her mother dug out every cleaning appliance and disinfectant they owned. They stripped the beds and vacuumed the carpet, scrubbed the bathroom and scoured the kitchen counter-tops. Cassie brought down fresh linens and some food for the refrigerator. *Faye and Laurel will be pleased*, Cassie thought. As far as overnight hiding places went, this was a best-case scenario.

When they were finished, Cassie's mother gave her an affectionate squeeze and headed back upstairs. Cassie's mind turned to her father's book. She had to figure out where it was.

She eyed the mysterious room. Her mother was so good at keeping secrets—too good. How would Cassie ever discover where she'd hidden the book? It could be anywhere.

And then the answer unwrapped itself like a gift. The room was spelled for protection, which meant Cassie could safely perform a summoning spell to locate the book without fear of being caught by her mother—or the hunters.

She listened for a moment to be sure there was no movement coming from upstairs and then tightly closed her eyes. She concentrated and whispered a simple incantation:

Book of Shadows, I summon thee.
Be released, appear to me.

Nothing happened at first, but then Cassie felt a peculiar tugging at her throat, a pull from the necklace around her neck. She grasped its silver chain, quickly released its clasp, and held it out in front of her. The quivering pendant was clear quartz. Of course—it was a visionary stone. It must have begun picking up traces of the book's energy.

Cassie let the pendant hang from its silver chain and watched the delicate crystal spin until it aligned itself in a definite direction. Soon it started swinging in broad sweeping strokes, like a pendulum.

Cassie took careful steps in the direction it led, keeping her hand steady as best she could. She followed the curve of its path, which was guiding her nowhere near the room's exit but toward the couch in the sitting area. Was it possible her mother had hidden the book down here in the basement? A strange excitement filled Cassie's chest as the silver chain straightened to a thin vertical line. The crystal stopped moving. It pointed and quaked at the floor directly below Cassie's feet.

Excitedly, Cassie lifted the throw rug to reveal the pale wooden slabs of flooring beneath it. There was a slight crack in one of the panels, barely visible to the eye but just large enough to dig out with her fingernail. It took a few tries to lift the board out of place, but once it was removed, the others were simple. And there was the book, nestled within a carefully carved divot like a tomb.

Cassie eyed the dark book like a dormant enemy. She leaned in close to it and poked it with her pointer finger. Then, deciding it was safe to pick up, she held it in her hands.

She couldn't have Faye and Laurel lounging around so close to something so private and powerful. She wasn't so concerned about Laurel using it, but *Faye*. She had to make sure Faye didn't discover this book under any circumstances. The secret room was definitely no place for it.

Cassie replaced the floorboards and the rug, then stood up to make her way to the stairs. She held the book close to her chest, trying to decide if she could sneak it past her mother by hiding it beneath her shirt. And then out of nowhere a foreign and mysterious feeling passed over her. She looked down at the book in her hands and had the overwhelming urge to open it, right then and there. She couldn't say why. She was sure it would burn her again, but her desire for even that brutal punishment was so strong, it was like a craving. The need came from somewhere deep inside her.

She looked around the room and listened for her mother's footsteps upstairs. No one would know. Not her mother, not the Circle. It would be her own secret—all her own.

The book seemed to be calling her, beckoning her.

But Cassie thought back to her mother's warnings, and shook her head to resist the urge. She quickly shoved the book under her shirt and ran upstairs to her bedroom before she had the chance to change her mind.

She would wait until Adam was with her to open it—that was the smart thing to do. Until then she would conceal the book out of sight. She knew just the place: Beneath her bed was a gunmetal chest that locked with a key. Cassie kneeled down, pulled it out into the light, and stuffed the book inside. It pained her to let go of the book when she so badly wanted it near her, but she forced herself to slam the chest closed, lock it, and shove it back underneath her bed.

The golden key to the chest felt warm in the palm of Cassie's hand. She squeezed it tightly in her fist, realizing she would have to hide it in a separate place. She decided on her old wooden jewelry box, which had a hidden pull-out bottom nobody knew about. Cassie gently placed the key inside, just beside the chalcedony rose Adam had given her. *The two of them can keep an eye on each other,* she thought, and then realized how ridiculous that was. Inanimate objects didn't live and breathe. Right?

CHAPTER 5

It was the middle of the night, dark and quiet, when Cassie unlocked the gunmetal chest and reached inside for her father's Book of Shadows. She held the book close to her face, and took a deep breath in. It smelled musty and old. She ran her palm over its soft, faded cover and traced its inscription with her finger. She wanted to absorb every detail. Finally, she pressed her thumb onto the worn oval on its corner—Black John's fingerprint—and found it was a perfect fit.

Cassie knew what she was doing was wrong. She'd promised herself she wouldn't open the book without Adam. But she couldn't control her own hands. They shook with excitement as she flipped through the book's yellowed pages. The words printed there still appeared as wavy lines and ancient symbols, but they were somehow more familiar to her. She could sense their meaning; she could almost taste it. And as she continued scanning each page, from top to bottom, left to right, she could feel herself getting sucked into the book itself, like she was becoming a part of it and it a part of her. That dark feeling she was beginning to know so well filled her stomach, and then her heart. Soon it was shivering provocatively through her whole body.

With a final shudder, Cassie startled awake. All was still and silent in her room. It was just a bad dream, she thought, but a painful throbbing ran from the tips of her fingers up the length of her wrists.

Cassie reached over to her lamp on the nightstand and found she could barely grip the switch to turn it on. But when she did, the light revealed an alarming sight: The marks on her hands had deepened to a shocking crimson. And, Cassie noticed, there was a dark red, cruel-looking welt on the inside of her left palm. It was a new mark.

But the book was locked away—there was no way Cassie could have actually touched it. Could she?

She ducked under her bed to check for the gunmetal

chest. She'd positioned it just so, perfectly aligned with a faint line on the floorboard, so she could easily tell if someone discovered and tampered with it.

The chest was in place with its lock still fastened. Next, Cassie checked her jewelry box. The key was there, lying innocently beside the chalcedony rose, just as she'd left it.

But Cassie was sure she'd had the book in her hands—how else could these new marks be explained? And she was positive she'd actually been reading the book. She *felt* different. A strange energy surged through her veins. It felt like strength, like capability. Like power.

⁓⁓⁓⁓⁓⁓

Cassie woke up the next morning to find her mother pulling open the curtains in her room, filling it with bright sunlight. "You were really in a deep sleep," her mother said. "You snored right through your alarm."

Cassie glanced down at her burned hands and hid them beneath the bedspread.

"Your friends came by about an hour ago," her mother continued. "But I sent them home."

Cassie sat up and tried to get her bearings. "You sent them home? We were supposed to have a Circle meeting."

"You seemed to need your rest more." Her mother

patted Cassie aside and sat next to her. "I went ahead and told your friends about the secret room in the basement. And I already spoke to Faye's mother and Laurel's guardians about letting them spend their nights here. Everything's all set. That's one less thing for you to worry about."

Cassie's mouth was dry and her mind was still groggy, but she was awake enough to understand that her mother was supporting her in a whole new way. She had basically sat in on Cassie's Circle meeting for her and single-handedly accomplished everything on the agenda. Her mother, the same woman who had refused to even utter the word *witchcraft* one year earlier. "And another thing," her mom said. "You and your friends are going to the spring dance. It's been decided."

For a second Cassie thought she might be dreaming again, but then she noticed her mother's sly smile. "Really," Cassie said. "The Circle decided that. And I'm sure you played no part in convincing them."

"Guilty as charged." Her mother raised up her hands, defenseless. "I think you all deserve a break. And it'll be a good reminder that you're in high school—these are supposed to be the best years of your life."

True, Cassie thought. She was in high school, but

she also had people's lives in her hands. Not to mention her own.

"Are you hungry?" her mother asked, changing the subject before Cassie could protest the dance. "You must be, it's already lunchtime. I'll fix us something to eat."

She was already through the door headed for the kitchen when Cassie called out to her. "Mom—thank you." Cassie knew just how lucky she was, not only to have a mother—unlike most of her friends—but to have *her* mother.

"Mmhmm," her mother replied modestly, like it was nothing at all.

Cassie let her head drop back onto her pillow. Her mind immediately began to spin. She needed to tell Adam about the dream she had had last night, if it had been a dream at all. Even now, as exhausted as she felt, Cassie had the urge to grab the book and search its pages for anything resembling the witch-hunter curse.

Cassie reached for her cell phone to quickly text Adam: *What are you up to? Can you come over?*

He instantly wrote back: *Can't. Taking Grandma to doctor, remember? But I'll see you tonight.*

That's right. She knew Adam was busy today, but they'd made plans to have the evening to themselves.

Where was her head? The restless night had left her brain foggy and confused.

A night alone with Adam was exactly what Cassie needed. In addition to everything about the book and the dream, there was something even more overwhelming weighing on Cassie's mind: She had to talk to Adam about the cord she'd seen connecting Adam to Scarlett on the night Scarlett left town. Whether or not Adam had seen it, and whether or not talking about it would be like throwing a hammer through the glass window of their relationship, it had to be addressed tonight. There could be no more secrets between them.

Cassie crawled out of bed and headed toward the sweet smells wafting from the kitchen. She'd better eat; she'd need her strength later.

———————

Faye and Laurel appeared at Cassie's front door that afternoon with suitcases in tow. "Pop the champagne," Faye said sarcastically as she stepped inside. "We're here to prepare for our extended slumber party."

Laurel sped past her and asked where the secret room was. She obviously didn't want to waste any time with small talk.

"Follow me," Cassie said. She was still feeling shaken

up from her nightmare and had hoped the doorbell would be Adam arriving early, but for Faye's and Laurel's sake she tried to sound pleasant. She also did her best to keep her burns covered, though that was becoming more and more challenging. The sleeves of her shirts were getting stretched out from constantly pulling them down over her hands.

"This feels like something out of an Edgar Allan Poe story," Faye said as Cassie led them downstairs and through the basement. "Wasn't he a fan of burying people alive?"

Laurel nodded. "In catacombs. Subterranean receptacles of the dead."

"I think you'll have a change of heart when you see it," Cassie said.

When they reached the bookcase, Cassie explained how it worked as a secret door. Then she closed her eyes, focused her energy on the wall of books, and recited the words her mother had used: "Enchanted threshold, door untold, reveal to me what you conceal."

Surprise flashed across Faye's and Laurel's faces the moment the doorway appeared in the bookshelf.

"Your grandmother was a sneaky lady," Faye said. "A woman of my own kind."

Laurel stepped inside the room and picked up a plush

throw pillow from the sofa. "It's like Victorian England in here."

"I'm glad you like it." Cassie smiled. "I want you both to be comfortable."

"It certainly has less of a bomb-shelter feel than I expected," said Faye. Cassie knew that was the closest thing to a compliment she was going to get.

Faye claimed her side of the room and immediately began taking things out of her suitcase and spreading them around—some candles and perfume bottles, her makeup case, her favorite jewelry.

"What we should be doing," Faye said, as she arranged her nail polishes and lipsticks upon the dresser by color, "is taking action against Max and his dad. I don't understand what we're waiting for."

"We *are* taking action." Cassie tried to sound patient but firm. "But it's important for you two to keep under the radar as best you can."

"It's not fair," Laurel blurted out. She was standing over her closed suitcase, not as quick to settle in as Faye.

"I know," Cassie said, as sympathetically as she could. "But I promise you, Laurel, we'll do what we have to do. In the meantime, keeping close to the Circle is the best way to truly be safe."

"I still want to go to the Spring Fling tomorrow night," Faye said, without looking up from her tincture collection. The tiny vials ranged from innocuous-looking browns to malicious purples. "The rest of the Circle will be there. There's no reason Laurel and I should have to miss it."

Cassie didn't bat an eye. "You're free to go to the dance if you want to. But Mr. Boylan and Max will be there, too, and there'll only be a handful of chaperones guarding an endless number of dark hallways. Need I remind you of Jeffrey Lovejoy hanging dead in the boiler room the night of the homecoming dance last year? Is that what you want to happen to you, Faye?"

Cassie didn't realize until a moment too late that she'd been yelling. Her face and neck felt flushed and she'd broken into a sweat.

Faye was so caught off guard by Cassie's eruption, her only response was stunned silence. Laurel backed away from her, awestruck.

Cassie's hands were balled into fists. When she released them, the burns on her skin tingled.

"Cassie's right," Laurel said, still eyeing Faye with an expression of alarm. "Forget the stupid dance. We'll hang out here and watch a movie. Your pick."

Faye simply nodded, which was a more agreeable

gesture than Cassie thought she was capable of. It wasn't like Faye to let anyone off easy, and Cassie was grateful for it.

"I'm sorry," Cassie said, trying to inject a new calm into her voice. "I didn't mean to snap at you like that."

Faye returned to her suitcase and resumed unpacking, but she refused to look Cassie in the eye.

"Faye," Cassie said, softening her voice further. "I don't know what came over me. I think I'm just on edge with everything going on."

It was the best she could do for a peace offering, but Faye wasn't taking the bait.

"It's okay, Cassie," Laurel said. She'd finally opened her suitcase and had begun removing her things, laying them out neatly on the dresser. "None of us feel like ourselves these days."

Faye sprayed her neck and wrists with perfume and then rubbed them together. "I feel just fine," she said, as the air around her grew heavy with the perfume's invigorating scent. "Better than fine, in fact. Unlike some people, I'm in complete control of myself."

She glanced at Cassie at last, as if she were deciding to pursue an argument or let it go.

"I guess you're a stronger person than I am," Cassie

said, knowing that was the one thing she could say to make Faye feel better.

And it did. After a few seconds, Faye's eyebrows relaxed and she said, "At least you're willing to admit that."

Then she moved to her bed, opened her laptop, and asked, "Can we at least get Wi-Fi down here?"

Cassie smiled. "I think that's the least I can do." And just like that, she'd been forgiven for her outburst.

CHAPTER 6

"I know we said this would be our evening alone, but Raj has been suffering from some major separation anxiety lately." Adam was on Cassie's doorstep with a pizza box in one hand and a dog leash in the other.

"It's okay." Cassie bent down to give the shaggy dog a loving pat. "We're not completely alone with Jekyll and Hyde downstairs anyway. At least Raj can't order me around like a maidservant."

Adam's eyes softened. "Has it gotten that bad already?" he asked, nodding in the direction of Faye and Laurel in the basement.

"Let's just say I'd love to take this pizza to go."

"A picnic on the bluff. That's a great idea. Let's do it." Adam tugged on Raj's leash and the dog sniffed and snorted, almost too excited for Adam to keep hold of him.

Cassie grabbed a jacket and followed Adam out the door. Of course it was impossible for Faye and Laurel to hear her, but Cassie still couldn't bring herself to open up to Adam about her nightmare or the cord with her friends so close by. Whether it was pure paranoia or not, having a heart-to-heart with Adam out in the fresh air on the bluff seemed like a far superior option.

Adam kept Raj in check as he and Cassie made their way along Crowhaven Road, arm in arm, savoring the beautiful night. Cassie felt safe and protected with Adam, but she couldn't help surveying the surrounding area, scanning every tree and shadow, alert to any movement or sound. She knew Scarlett or a hunter could be behind any one of the many crooked mailboxes or lopsided lamp-posts along their way.

The bluff was tranquil, a rocky fort of solitude. The night was quiet in a way that usually made Cassie feel calm, but tonight she wanted to scream as loud as she could and shatter it.

Adam instructed Raj to lie down, then opened up the

pizza box and handed Cassie a drooping, dripping slice. "I got your favorite. Hawaiian."

Cassie accepted the slice from him and took a small bite before diving right into what she'd been waiting to say. "I have to tell you something," Cassie said. Her words echoed into the night. "I had a dream last night."

"By the tone of your voice," Adam said while chewing, "I'm guessing it wasn't a good one."

Cassie shook her head. "And it was so real. I'm not sure if it actually happened."

"If it was a dream, Cassie, of course it didn't happen. Are you saying you had another vision? Was it Scarlett?"

"No. This was something else." Cassie looked down from the sloping cliff to the lapping water below. "In the dream I was reading my father's Book of Shadows, absorbing all of its energy. And then when I woke up my hands had been burned. See this?"

Cassie set her slice of pizza down and lifted her shirt-sleeve to show Adam the new burn on the inside of her hand. "That wasn't there before I went to bed."

Adam closely examined the mark. "Okay, that's weird," he said. "Do you think you were reading the book in your sleep?"

Cassie pulled her sleeve back down and picked at a

pineapple bit on top of her pizza. "I don't know. When I woke up, I found it locked away just as I'd left it before I went to bed. It really doesn't make any sense."

"Have you told anyone else about this?"

"No, just you. And I want to keep it that way."

Adam's face took on an air of seriousness as his eyes wandered across the bluff. Cassie could tell he was trying to come up with some explanation or solution, but not finding any.

"We have to find out more about that book," he said. "It's time for us to learn how dark magic works."

Cassie stiffened at the words *dark magic*. It wasn't something she wanted to be associated with, especially in Adam's mind. But Adam was right.

"I want to try to open the book," Cassie said. "With you at my side. I know for sure the witch-hunter curse my father used is in there and I want us to research it together."

"I think that's a good idea." Adam put aside his half-eaten slice of pizza and held Cassie by the shoulders. "I understand your fears about telling the rest of the Circle about this, but they might be able to help. Diana's Book of Shadows has a lot of information in it. We should at least tell her, if not the others."

Cassie shook her head. "Not yet."

"Diana's not going to judge you," Adam said. "You know that."

"There's more to it than that, Adam."

Cassie could see how strongly Adam disagreed with her, so she had to remain firm. "This is a private matter," she said. "A family matter. It's not for you to decide who should and shouldn't know about it."

"Fine." Adam exhaled loudly. "When you're ready then."

For a few seconds his frustration was palpable. He got quiet and picked a pebble off the ground, worrying it between his fingers.

But soon enough he lobbed the pebble into the water and refocused on Cassie. "I'm with you on this," he said. "I need you to know that."

Cassie reached out to pull Adam closer. She buried her head in his chest and he rested his chin on her hair. Raj barked and jumped with jealousy. He nosed at their legs and pawed at their feet until Cassie gave in and bent down to give him a pat on the head. Adam laughed and stroked the dog's disheveled coat.

"I think Raj is right," Adam said. "We've had enough serious talk for one night." He returned to his pizza and bit off a mouthful.

"Actually, there's one more thing." Cassie looked down at the dewy ground. As much as she wanted to forget all her troubles and enjoy her time with Adam, she knew she couldn't keep the cord a secret from him any longer.

"More bad news?" Adam said with a smile. "Have you been saving it all up for this one walk?"

"Kind of." Cassie couldn't bear to fake levity. "I've kept this inside for a while now."

Adam commanded Raj to sit and tried to read Cassie's expression. "What is it?"

"I saw something," Cassie said, in a barely audible voice. "That night in Cape Cod. When I was in your arms. I saw the cord, our cord."

"Okay."

"But I also saw a second cord. Going from you to Scarlett."

"I don't understand what you're telling me," Adam said, but Cassie knew he must have perfectly understood what she was saying.

"It looked just like ours," Cassie explained. "But it was between the two of you. What do you think that means?"

Adam shook his head. "I didn't see anything like that."

Cassie didn't want this to turn into an argument, but denying it wouldn't help any. They couldn't just pretend this away. "I saw it with my own eyes," she said. "I could almost reach out and touch it."

"Cassie." Adam took Cassie's face into his hands and made her look him in the eye. "Whatever conclusion your mind is racing to right now, stop it. You were close to dying when you think you saw that cord. You must have been hallucinating in the smoke."

"Adam . . ." Cassie started to say, but he interrupted.

"The silver cord is just between us. That's how soul mates work."

"What if you have more than one soul mate? That's what I'm asking."

"I don't even think that's possible." Adam wrapped his arms around Cassie's torso. "And any cord aside, I love you, Cassie. Only you. With everything I have."

"I love you too, but—"

Adam kissed Cassie on the mouth, softly at first and then with more passion. The kisses made Cassie feel dizzy and light-headed in a way that made her want to giggle out loud. Even more so, she felt him—his essence—intertwining with hers.

Then Adam abruptly pulled away. "Did you feel that?"

"Of course I did."

"That's all the proof I need. Cord or no cord. So forget about what you think you saw when you were half-conscious." Adam kissed Cassie again, this time affectionately on the cheek.

His lips felt warm and loving on her skin, and she couldn't deny the feeling she got every time Adam kissed her. He was right about that much.

"I only wish you'd told me this sooner," he said. "I hate that you've been worrying about this."

"You would tell me if you saw it, wouldn't you, Adam?" Cassie wasn't sure where the question came from. She never doubted Adam's word before. She'd never had a reason to.

But Adam hesitated in a way that caught her attention. His answer didn't come with the immediacy of honesty.

"Of course I'd tell you," he said, calmly and dismissively, only after he'd faltered. "I didn't see a thing. And I don't think you did either."

Perhaps it was all in Cassie's head, but Adam didn't sound quite convincing enough. Maybe she was even more confused and paranoid than she realized.

Cassie turned away, focusing her attention on the long murky line of Crowhaven houses in the distance

behind them. Like Adam said, cord aside, their relationship had grown and evolved way beyond love at first
sight.

"You know what I think?" Adam said in a lighter
tone. "I think it's time you allowed yourself to relax. Your
mother's right—you're taking on too much."

"She said that to you?"

Adam nodded. "At the meeting you slept through
this morning. But she didn't have to. We can all see
it, Cassie. And you're not alone." Cassie started to
respond, but Adam got that goofy look on his face once
more.

"Will you do me the honor of being my date for
the Spring Fling? We could use a little fun, hunters be
damned. And I can't think of a better person to have on
my arm than you."

Cassie giggled in spite of herself. But her gaze shifted
back to Crowhaven Road, all the way down to the blackened depths of the bottom of the hill. "That sounds
perfect, but I don't know if we can afford to make fun a
priority right now."

Then Cassie paused and thought better of the idea.
"On second thought," she said, "the dance might be just
the opportunity we need to get close to the principal and

Max in a public setting, to see if we can figure out some of their weaknesses, or find out more about their stone relics."

"Cassie. You're missing the point. Your only concern should be making sure I wear the right color bow tie."

"Come on, Adam, I know you better than that. You're always putting Circle business first, before everything else."

Adam blushed with guilt. "Okay, you're right. Using the dance to get close to the hunters had crossed my mind. But that is all the more reason we both need a night off." His eyes flickered in the moonlight and he reached for Cassie's hand. "No magic. Just go to the dance and have a nice time—simple as that."

Adam was so much better than Cassie at being happy these days. Maybe some awful punch and silly dancing with her friends and boyfriend was just what she needed to clear out the black cloud that had settled into her chest. At the very least she could pretend to be excited about it—for Adam's sake, and her mother's peace of mind.

Cassie accepted Adam's hand and let him draw her in, ballroom dance–style.

"Pink," she whispered into his ear. "For your bow tie."

Adam took a step back. "Seriously? Couldn't you choose a color that's a bit more manly?"

"Nope. Pink it is."

CHAPTER 7

For a dance in the school gymnasium, the Spring Fling wasn't bad. The walls were camouflaged with cheerful decorations and multicolored streamers. Twinkling lights hung from the ceiling like shooting stars. The basketball hoops were tied back and filled with bright, pungent flowers—primroses, tulips, and chrysanthemums—masking the smell of adolescent sweat. The gym had been completely transformed.

As promised, Adam had matched his bow tie to Cassie's pink halter dress perfectly. She fiddled with its knot now, straightening it solely as an excuse to touch him.

"Would you get me a glass of punch?" she asked. "Or else I might have to start kissing you."

Adam grinned. "I'll be right back."

Cassie stood alone for a moment and gazed around the gymnasium. Everyone from the Circle had come except for Faye and Laurel, and Melanie, who thought Laurel would need moral support being cooped up with Faye. Cassie thought about giving them a call to check in and see how they were doing, but then Nick appeared before her.

"You look beautiful," he said.

He'd caught Cassie by surprise, so she laughed, embarrassed. "Thank you. You don't look half bad yourself."

Nick stared down at himself, wearing his regular jeans, T-shirt, and leather jacket. "I didn't really dress for the occasion," he said. "But this is a clean shirt, so I guess that's something."

Cassie laughed again and a sudden warmth came to her cheeks.

"Do you feel like dancing?" Nick asked.

Cassie hesitated.

An air of mischief crept into Nick's face. "I'm only asking because I know you, Cassie Blake, came here with a very specific mission to have some fun tonight. I couldn't let you go home a failure."

"Then how could I possibly say no?" Cassie allowed Nick to lead her onto the dance floor.

Whatever song the band was playing was loud and boisterous, nothing Cassie recognized, but it felt good to let her guard down and just enjoy the music—to enjoy the simple pleasure of being a girl at a dance. Nick skipped and bopped about trying to amuse her. She knew he actually hated dancing and that this was all for her benefit. Cassie appreciated the effort and followed his lead, synchronizing her steps to his until together they were making quite a scene.

From the dance floor Cassie saw that Adam had returned with her punch, and Diana was behind him with a glass for herself.

Nick dashed for them, took the cups from their hands to set them aside, and then pulled them onto the dance floor, too. Deborah and Suzan were quick to join in, and before Cassie knew it, Nick had single-handedly altered the energy of the whole group. They were all being silly, rambunctiously bumping into their classmates on the dance floor, infuriating them in the process. It made Cassie remember when she and Nick were together, and how sometimes his refusal to take anything seriously was just the thing she needed to get out of her own head and start having a good time.

Then the music changed to a slow song—one of

Cassie's favorites. She looked at Adam, hoping he would ask her to dance, but she noticed his attention was elsewhere. He was watching someone.

"Max is here," he said. "Act natural."

"Whatever that means," Nick mumbled under his breath. He turned around and cut through the crowd toward the punch bowl. Their merriment was nothing more than a lingering memory.

"It's supposed to be our night off," Suzan said, pouting. "Remember? No policing tonight."

But Cassie knew it was only a matter of time before the Spring Fling became about Circle business, just like everything else. Come to think of it, she was surprised it had taken this long. The group dutifully exited the dance floor and gathered near the back wall.

Max sauntered over to them with his usual air of confidence. He was dressed in a black shirt, black pants, and a necktie as brilliantly green as his eyes. "Hey," he said, greeting Diana first, as always. "Is Faye around? I can't find her."

"Didn't she tell you?" Diana said. "Faye's got a terrible cold."

"Oh," Max said, disappointed. "No, I didn't know. She hasn't answered any of my calls." When Max pouted, his features softened, bringing out the boyish charm to his face.

Diana frowned sympathetically. "Don't take it personally. She's been knocked out on decongestants since yesterday. I bet she turned her phone off."

Cassie couldn't tell if Max was buying Diana's story or not. She thought he looked more confused than skeptical, but Diana must have sensed some suspicion in him because she didn't stop there.

"Just because Faye's not here doesn't mean your night should be ruined," Diana said to him.

Max cracked a sideways, hopeful smile.

"Dance with me," Diana said. And before Max could even react, she grabbed him by the arm and hurried him to the dance floor. The band was still playing a slow song, so Diana clasped her arms around the back of Max's neck and let him hold her lower back.

Max gazed into Diana's eyes as if he couldn't believe his good fortune. All his arrogance and swagger had given way to a sturdy modesty, and he held Diana with care. Faye was the furthest thing from his mind, Cassie was sure of that.

"I know we want to keep an eye on Max," Adam said. "But this is ridiculous."

Cassie noticed Adam's jaw tighten as he watched the couple dance. Diana was laughing, squeezing Max close, having what appeared to be a pretty good time. Cassie wouldn't dare say so to Adam, but she couldn't help but sense Diana wasn't thinking about the Circle anymore.

A few minutes later, Chris, Doug, and Sean turned up at Cassie's side.

"Do you see what I see?" Chris asked, and Cassie followed his gaze to the opposite side of the gym.

It was Mr. Boylan, standing with his arms crossed in a finely cut dark suit, his gaze locked on Max and Diana on the dance floor.

"He looks like he's about to kill someone," Doug said. "What should we do?"

Just then Mr. Boylan turned the other way and stormed out of the gym.

"Follow him," Cassie said.

The three of them—Chris, Doug, and Sean—bolted toward the exit without a moment's hesitation. Cassie saw from the look on his face that Adam was anxious to join them.

"This is my chance to search Mr. Boylan's office," he said. "For his relic."

So much for a night off, Cassie thought. But if Adam

could steal Boylan's relic from him it would be the equivalent of robbing him of his power. He couldn't perform the killing curse without it.

Cassie grazed Adam's cheek with her hand and nodded. "It's a good idea, but you shouldn't go alone. You'll need a lookout."

"We'll go," Deborah said. She and Suzan stepped forward, a little too anxiously. "We've been itching for something interesting to happen all night. Or at least I have." She acknowledged Suzan, who was still sulking about being pulled from the dance floor.

"Be careful," Cassie said, as if it were an order. She was still a Circle leader, after all. "I'll keep an eye on Diana and Max."

Adam gave Cassie's hand a squeeze and then took off. Deborah and Suzan followed him toward the hallway that led to Mr. Boylan's office. Cassie allowed herself a moment to breathe, to remind herself that though everything was suddenly happening so fast, it was all under control. Her control. Then Nick materialized from the crowd with another glass of punch for Cassie.

"I'm pretty sure it's not spiked," he said. "But at this rate I think we can both at least count on a sugar high." Then he noticed the expression on Cassie's face. "What's going on?" His dark brown eyes darted back and forth. "Where is everyone?"

"Chris, Doug, and Sean are tailing Boylan. Adam, Deborah, and Suzan are searching his office."

"I thought we were here to take it easy," Nick said.

"Change of plan." Cassie scoped the gymnasium for Diana's blond hair and Max's broad shoulders, but they'd gotten lost in the swarm of students. "Do you see Diana anywhere?"

Nick inspected every couple on the dance floor then shook his head. "It's too crowded. But I have an idea." He ran to the punch table and, to the dismay of the servers, climbed up on top of it for a better view. He scanned the room back and forth and then he froze in place. His sharp features turned deathly serious.

"Cassie," he whispered, and jumped down. But before he could utter another word, Cassie caught sight of a wild mane of dyed-red hair. It was no hallucination this time. No paranoia. Right in the center of the crowd was Scarlett.

Nick looked ready to pounce, but he didn't move a muscle. "She's casting a spell," he said.

Scarlett's arms were rigid at her sides and her eyes were as black as marbles. She was muttering something under her breath, obviously some kind of dark magic.

"We have to get you out of here," Nick said. "Right now!"

Cassie was smart enough not to argue. She and Nick rushed toward the nearest exit, but suddenly everyone around them started to act odd. Their necks went soft and their heads drooped down. Their classmates had all fallen into a stupor.

Nick shot a look at Cassie. "What the heck is going on?" He positioned himself between Cassie and the nearest group blocking the exit.

Whatever Scarlett was doing seemed to be affecting everyone but Cassie and Nick. But it soon became clear that their classmates were simply collateral damage. With them out of the way, Scarlett now had a clear shot at her intended target. She redirected all her wicked mumbling straight at Cassie:

Spirant ultimus spiritus
Ultimus spiritus vitae

Suddenly all the air rushed out of Cassie's lungs and she couldn't inhale any more in. It was like a clamp had fastened around her throat, blocking her breath. She brought her hands to her neck and turned to Nick. There was no breath to enable a scream.

Nick ran to her as if it were a simple piece of food lodged in her throat, as if the Heimlich maneuver could save her—but there was nothing he could do. And with their stupefied classmates crowding every exit, there was no way to escape.

Cassie's head spun from the lack of oxygen. She reached out for Nick as she fell to the gymnasium floor.

CHAPTER 8

Nick screamed Cassie's name. He was bent over her, trying to get her to breathe, but Cassie could feel herself losing consciousness with each second that passed. The yellow gymnasium light, their comatose classmates, and even Scarlett's wicked voice had blended into a soft, shadowy haze. Then Nick stood up and raised his arms with outstretched hands.

No! Cassie tried to cry out—the worst thing Nick could do right now was perform magic out in the open— but no sound escaped her gaping mouth.

Nick centered his energy, closed his eyes, and made his voice deep:

*I call on the Power of Air, the element from
the East, I call you from the atmosphere to
Cassie's lungs.*

He repeated the spell three times, louder each moment, but Cassie continued to fade out of consciousness. The whole world diffused; sound ceased. There was nothing. And then all at once she gasped like a drowned woman resuscitated, reclaiming her life with one greedy breath after another.

Her vision sharpened with each inhalation, and she climbed to her feet just as Nick raised his hands to call out another spell—this time not at Cassie, but up at the ceiling:

*Motion of heart, current of soul, spark
to my hands, at the speed of light.*

His face took on a lustrous glow and electricity seemed to pass through him, up from his feet and out of his fingertips.

The overhead bulbs flashed and then burst, raining down spectacular long-tailed sparks like fireworks. Then the gym went black as night.

"Run," Nick said, grabbing Cassie's hand.

Their stupefied classmates panicked in the sudden darkness. Cassie could no longer see them, but she could hear them grunting and groaning. Their elbows and knees knocked against the gym floor as they tumbled over one another in a massive stampede.

Cassie and Nick raced through the maze of bodies, heading for the emergency exit, without once looking back to see what had become of Scarlett. They stormed through the fire door out to the side parking lot, where they ran straight into the rest of the Circle.

"Are you all right?" Diana asked in alarm. "What just happened in the gym?"

Nick and Cassie hurriedly explained the situation and Diana's mouth dropped open. "Scarlett's here?"

Both Henderson brothers bolted back to the gym to find her. Cassie screamed for them not to, but they were already gone.

"Someone has to stop them," she cried out. "They'll get themselves killed."

"I'll go," Deborah said, taking off in the same direction as the Hendersons. Suzan followed just behind her.

Diana searched Cassie for any sign of an injury. "Are you sure you're okay? You aren't hurt?"

Cassie nodded. "I'm fine. I think we got out just in time. Where's Adam?"

"Right here." Adam walked up to the group, looking pale. His hands were trembling slightly and they were empty of Mr. Boylan's relic. "Cassie," he said. "Have you been out here long?"

"I'm okay," Cassie said to reassure him.

Adam appeared more shaken than she was. His breathing was heavy and his forehead was soaked with sweat. He scanned the surrounding area with apprehension.

"Scarlett's nowhere to be found," Chris called out as he and Doug exited the gym to rejoin the group. Deborah and Suzan were alongside him.

"The lights are still out, but everyone in the gym is back to normal," Doug said. "Which is too bad, really. I kind of liked the idea of them all being zombified."

Cassie looked at Nick, happy he was okay. He was so quick to react, and he'd saved her life, but she never intended for him to be in danger like that. Especially with Mr. Boylan and Max around.

Nick returned her gaze. He seemed to understand exactly what she was thinking and he smiled reassuringly for her. It was just then that Cassie saw something glisten on the sleeve of his leather jacket. It was dim at first, but once she noticed it, it appeared to shine more clearly. It was the hunter symbol.

"Nick," she said, but that was the only word she could get out.

He registered Cassie's expression and then watched everyone else's face fall into the same shock.

"What?" he asked. "Why do you all look like you've seen a ghost?"

"Your sleeve," Diana said. "You've been marked."

Cassie went to him, but Nick shook her off. He searched his jacket and located the mark. He concentrated hard on it, squinting as if trying to understand it, but had no other reaction.

"So I have," he said, in a voice as still and cold as stone.

Adam barely said a word the whole car ride home to Cassie's. Cassie didn't take it personally; she didn't feel much like making conversation either. What was there to say after an evening like this? But when Adam parked in front of her house, he cut the engine and turned to her like he had something to get off his chest.

"Are you sure you don't want me to stay on your couch for the night?" he asked. "Scarlett might still be coming after you."

There was a chill in the air that made Cassie shiver. "Thank you," she said. "But I'll be okay. Faye and Laurel are there, and Faye wouldn't miss the chance to act on some of her anger if Scarlett showed up."

"That's true, I guess." Adam tapped his fingers on the steering wheel.

Cassie was wearing his suit jacket draped over her shoulders to keep warm. She went to take it off and give it back to him, but he stopped her.

"Keep it on a little longer," he said. He made no motion to restart the car's engine. Something else was obviously on his mind.

Cassie feared she knew what it was. Adam was concerned that Nick being marked would mean he'd have to start spending the night in Cassie's basement. The two of them would be sleeping under the same roof.

She decided to help him along. "Adam," she said. "About Nick staying here . . ."

Adam stared straight ahead. "It's not that," he said. "Can I ask you one more time what happened when the lights went out in the school?"

"I told you," Cassie said. "Nothing happened with Nick while you were gone that you need to worry about."

"I just need to hear it again."

Cassie had already given Adam a detailed account of her and Nick's every move from the moment they spotted Scarlett to their escape. But she repeated the story anyway.

"It's just so strange," he said, unable to look at her.

"Adam, what are you freaking out about? I know if you had been there when Scarlett showed up, you would have protected me, just like Nick did. I don't doubt that for a second."

Finally Adam turned to Cassie, allowing her to see his tearful eyes. "I felt something," he said. "An arm brushed up against mine in the chaos."

"What?" Cassie was confused.

"When the lights went out. I had just come out of Boylan's office and everyone started running. I was making my way toward the gym when someone grabbed my hand, and it felt like . . . I don't even know." Adam could barely continue, and Cassie began to understand just how upset he was.

"It's okay," she said, trying to coax the full truth out of him. "What did you feel?"

"I thought it was you leading me to safety, but then we got separated. I could have sworn it was you. Because of the sparks I felt."

"But I was already out of the gym and in the parking lot by that point," Cassie said. "It wasn't me."

There was a moment of silence as it all sank in.

"Oh," Cassie said, finally comprehending what this meant. Neither of them wanted to say it out loud, but it was obvious. It was Scarlett who'd grabbed Adam's hand. The sparks he felt were for her.

"It's you that I love, Cassie. I swear it." Adam's voice rose. "This doesn't mean anything."

"It means the cord between you and Scarlett must be real after all," Cassie said. "That's the only explanation."

"I shouldn't even have told you."

"Of course you should have told me!"

"This doesn't change anything." Adam persisted. But the more he swore and pleaded, the more obvious it was to Cassie that he was just as shaken by this as she was, if not more.

"My hand just got confused," he said. "That's all."

"Your hand got confused?" Cassie took an immediate breath to recalibrate her emotions. If she wasn't careful, her hurt and anger would blow up right in Adam's face.

"You don't have to feel guilty," she said, trying to sound sympathetic. "It's not your fault. It just is."

Adam got quiet then. "But I don't want this."

Cassie reached over to give Adam a kiss good night. She needed to get out of his car as quickly as possible. "I know," she said. "Don't worry too much about it. We'll be okay."

"That's it? Don't you think we should talk about this?" Adam asked.

Cassie slipped Adam's suit jacket from her shoulders. It smelled like him, like autumn leaves and ocean wind. She gently folded it and placed it on his lap. Then she put her hand on the door handle.

"It's going to be okay," she said, knowing she had to appear strong for Adam in this moment. Adam could always be relied on to reassure Cassie. Now it was her turn.

"Cassie, please don't go."

"Let's sleep on it," she said, as sweetly as she could. And then borrowing a favorite phrase of her mother's, she added, "Everything will look brighter tomorrow."

She got out of the car and almost made it to the front door before tears filled her eyes and began running down her face. But Adam couldn't see them, and that was all that mattered.

CHAPTER 9

After her encounter with Scarlett at the dance, Cassie's sleep was fitful—nightmare after nightmare plagued her mind. As she woke up, she knew what she had to do to make it stop. She pulled the gunmetal chest out from under her bed and unlocked its clasp. She'd wanted to wait for Adam to be with her before she tried to open the book again, but time was running out, and things with Adam had just gotten a whole lot more complicated. She couldn't allow a potential love triangle to trip up her search for answers.

Plus, she had an idea. In the jewelry box where she kept all her precious stones, Cassie had an obsidian crystal. It was the same crystal she'd once used to disable a guarding spell Faye had placed on one of the Master Tools. Cassie squeezed the sharp-edged black rock in her hand now. It was known to purify dark matter. Why not give it a try?

She glided the crystal over and around her father's Book of Shadows while whispering the chant that had been successful last time:

Darkness be gone, no shields are needed,
purity enters and leaves here unhindered.

Then she pulled on the book's leather string and fanned its cover open. She touched the first page hopefully, but it immediately grew hot, singeing the tip of her pointer finger.

Cassie drew back, but before the book flapped closed she thrust the obsidian crystal between its pages. At first the book struggled against the stone, rattling and thrashing, and the crystal shook over its pages like a kernel of corn in hot oil. But then the book seemed to tire. Slowly, each page grew calm and quiet beneath the crystal until they were still. The book's darkness had been tamed just enough to allow the rock to hold it open like a simple paperweight.

The words scrawled upon the first two pages still looked like an ancient language of lines and symbols. Viewing them this closely made Cassie's eyes feel strange and off kilter, like staring at an optical illusion. But at least now she could get to researching and translating. And if she maneuvered the obsidian just so, she could even use it to turn the book's pages. Wait till Adam saw this.

Just then her doorbell rang and Cassie realized what time it was. The Circle meeting to go over the events of the night before was set to begin in a few minutes. Cassie removed the obsidian and the book flapped closed. She quickly locked it back in its hiding place before running down to answer the door.

On her front porch was Nick, carrying a duffel bag over his shoulder. He didn't look happy, for obvious reasons, but Cassie was glad to have a moment with him before the rest of the Circle arrived.

She led him inside and asked him to have a seat on the living room sofa. "I'll show you downstairs in just a minute," she said. "But first I was hoping we could talk."

Nick dropped his bag on the floor and sat down. "Okay."

Cassie sat beside him. "I'm so sorry," she said. "I feel like it's my fault you got marked."

"Scarlett was trying to kill you. You weren't exactly asking for it," Nick said.

"I know, I just . . . you saved my life. And I can't bear to think what might happen to yours now."

Nick shook his head. "It's not your fault, Cassie. I knew the chance I was taking, and I chose to risk it. Besides, I can handle this."

Cassie reached for Nick's hand. It was a bold move, but she felt like under the circumstances it was worth the try.

For once he didn't pull away from her. Cassie opened her mouth to assure him that she would be there for him the way he was for her—but then a loud, pounding noise rattled the floor beneath them.

Nick jumped with alarm.

"It's okay," Cassie said. "It's only Faye and a broom handle. She finds the use of it ironic."

Nick tried to play it cool, but Cassie knew he was embarrassed about being so easily startled, that the cracks beneath his cool exterior were starting to show.

"It's Faye's special signal," she said casually. "When she bangs on the ceiling with the broom, it means she's in dire need of attention."

"When doesn't Faye need attention?" Nick ran his fingers through his hair and allowed himself to laugh. "So where *is* this secret room anyway?"

Cassie smiled. "Follow me."

She led Nick downstairs to the old bookshelves and cast the spell to reveal the hidden door. Faye and Laurel were waiting expectantly inside. They'd microwaved popcorn, baked cupcakes, and had music playing.

"I've been marked," Nick said, surveying the scene. "It's not my birthday." But he still reached for a pink-frosted cupcake and took a hearty bite.

The room had changed quite a bit since Cassie had last seen it. Faye and Laurel each infused it with their own character. Laurel's side of the room was draped with green plants, herbs, and flowers. Piles of thick books were stacked as high as the eye could see, many of them for the research she was doing on the hunters. Faye's side was adorned with red tapestries and velvety pillows. She'd also created a small altar that housed candles and incense and various concoctions.

"You'll have to carve out a space of your own," Cassie said to Nick. "At your own risk."

"I'll be just fine." Nick tossed his duffel bag down and shoved the last bite of cupcake into his mouth. "I don't need much."

"We've got an air mattress for you to sleep on," Faye said. "But if you get lonely, there's lots of extra room in my bed."

"Gross," Laurel shouted. "Not with me here there isn't."

"That's my cue to leave." Cassie let Nick get settled in and went upstairs to wait for the rest of the Circle to arrive for their meeting. As everyone trickled in, Cassie directed them downstairs. It was Adam she was really waiting for, but he was last to arrive, which was rare.

When he finally rambled up the walk, he appeared more disheveled than normal. His clothes were wrinkled and his hair was uncombed. There were dark circles beneath his eyes that made it look like he hadn't slept all night. Cassie hoped it wasn't yesterday's conversation about the cord weighing him down.

"Before we go downstairs," Adam said, "I want to show you something." He reached into the inside pocket of his jacket and retrieved a squeezable pink plastic tube.

"My lip gloss?" Cassie asked.

Adam nodded. "Not just any lip gloss. This fell out of your pocket the night of our first kiss. And this . . ."

Adam pulled a tiny square of paper from the same pocket. "This is the movie ticket stub from our official first date."

Next Adam held up his cell phone. "Saved on here," he said, "is the first time you said *I love you* to me on my voice mail. And these are only the beginning, Cassie. Do you understand what I'm getting at?"

"You're in great danger of becoming a hoarder?" Cassie grinned.

Adam laughed. "Maybe, but it's because everything and anything that reminds me of you, I have to save forever. If that doesn't prove that I'm head-over-heels in love with you, I don't know what will."

All the tension and fear Cassie built up overnight about their relationship had just floated up and away. She wanted to jump into Adam's arms and lose the afternoon in his embrace. But there was no time for that now. Their friends were waiting. All Cassie could do at the moment was kiss Adam with her whole being, and hope her love for him shined through, that their connection was palpable, before leading him downstairs to join the others.

"The hunters and Scarlett are way too close for comfort," Melanie was saying when Adam and Cassie entered the secret room.

Everyone was gathered in a circle except for Chris and Doug, who were stirring around in the kitchen like hyperactive children. Deborah agreed with Melanie. "We need to get closer to the hunters, to have full surveillance on them, since they're obviously watching us."

"I can get us closer to Max," Diana said.

Faye snickered and whispered something under her breath to Deborah and Suzan.

Diana turned to her. "I'm the only one who can easily do it," she said. "We all know that."

"But you could be putting yourself in danger," Faye said mockingly. Then her face took on a spiteful weightiness. "If given the chance, Max will mark you just like he did me."

Diana shrugged. "I'm not going to do any magic around him. Besides if I can get into his bedroom, I might be able to find out where he keeps his relic."

"You're not going anywhere near his bedroom," Faye shot back.

Laurel cleared her throat. "I've made some progress digging up information about the relics," she said. With a nod from Cassie, she took the center of the floor and explained to the Circle that the relics originated around 1320, shortly after Pope John XVII authorized the Inquisition to persecute witchcraft as a type of heresy.

"An accused witch created and spelled the relics in return for her life," Laurel said. "She christened the owners of these magical stones and taught them the killing curse."

"Of course they needed a witch to do their dirty work for them," Sean called out. "Wimps."

Laurel pursed her lips at the interruption. "Soon the Inquisition led to a wave of witch-hunting," she continued, "during which the relics were sighted throughout France, Italy, and Germany. But many of them were destroyed during the peak of the hunts, which occurred in the late 1500s till around 1630. And by the time the hunt reached Salem in the 1690s, only a dozen or so relics—and even fewer hunter families— had survived."

Laurel focused her eyes on Diana specifically. "It's now believed there are only six relics still active."

Diana was looking straight down at the floor. In almost a whisper she said, "That's all?"

Laurel glanced at Faye. "So it may be worth it for Diana to search Max's bedroom if it means we can bring that number down to five."

"Five, six, seven hundred, what difference does it make?" Nick called out. "We still don't have a way to beat them. Can we talk for a moment about Scarlett? She wants to kill Cassie, to get her spot in the Circle, and she has our Master Tools. She almost got the best of us last night, and she'll come back again. If we can't use magic on her, then we need to be ready to destroy her with our bare hands."

Deborah patted Nick on the shoulder. "Well, it goes without saying that my cousin can use some anger management right about now."

Until this point, everyone had been so engrossed in the discussion that no one had noticed Chris trying to squeeze his six-foot-tall body into the tiny confines of the dumbwaiter carved into the kitchen wall. But the racket he was creating finally captured the group's attention.

"I can do it," he said. "Doug, push my feet in for me. And then launch me upstairs."

Doug did as he was told, laughing. He shoved Chris's feet deeper into the box with one hand. His other hand hovered over the wooden lever that would send the dumbwaiter flying up the chute that led to the kitchen above them.

"Chris," Cassie yelled. "That'll never hold you. It's not an elevator. Get out before you break it."

"Don't mess with that thing," Faye called out to him. "It's our favorite way to have Cassie wait on us from upstairs."

"But I can do it," Chris said again. "I'm not as big as I look."

Cassie's patience had worn thin and a peculiar anger

surged through her. Her face and hands grew hot with rage. "I said, get out of there!"

Before she could get control of herself, she marched over to Doug and forcefully shoved him away from the lever. Her strength caught him by surprise, causing him to stumble backward.

Chris, in his struggle to climb out of the dumbwaiter before Cassie could reach him, slipped out headfirst and hit the floor with a thump.

A few silent seconds passed before he screamed out in pain, clutching his left arm.

"Now you've done it," Doug said. "You broke my brother."

"Seriously, Cassie," Sean said. "You didn't have to humiliate him like that."

"I barely touched him," Cassie screamed out.

"He's in pain," Diana said.

"Duh." Doug helped Chris to his feet. "I think his arm is broken."

"I guess Nick isn't the only one with anger issues." Deborah glanced at Cassie and then went to Chris's other side for support.

"He's in pain," Diana shouted out again. "Do you understand what this means?"

Cassie thought back to her car accident a few weeks ago, when she walked away unscathed, and she suddenly comprehended Diana's shock. "The protective spell is broken," Cassie said.

A spine-chilling quiet fell over the room as everyone realized what this meant for their safety.

"Scarlett in the gym last night," Diana said. "She wasn't there to ruin our dance. She was destroying the only thing keeping us alive."

CHAPTER 10

"*I figured out a way to open my father's book,*" Cassie said to Adam, pulling the gunmetal chest out from under her bed and the key from its hidden compartment in her jewelry box.

She had asked Adam to stay while the others accompanied Chris to the hospital. Now that the protection spell had been broken, they didn't have a moment to waste. They needed to end these hunters, once and for all.

"How?" he asked.

Cassie showed him the obsidian crystal and explained how it worked as a buffer to the book's dark energy. Cassie and Adam settled down on her bedroom floor, the book in front of them. Cassie opened it, knowing it would singe her fingers a bit before she could get the crystal in place, and it did. But once the rock had been set down, weighing upon the book's spine and clearing its energy, the book's first two pages were visible.

"This is incredible." Adam leaned over the book on his hands and knees, closely examining each brushstroke before him. "I recognize a few familiar symbols here. From my hunt for the Master Tools a while ago. Some of these same inscriptions were on Black John's map."

Cassie couldn't keep herself from smiling. "I was hoping you'd say something like that."

"I'll look back through my old research and see what I can find. Do you think we can take the book to my house?"

The idea of the book leaving her bedroom rattled Cassie and she faltered. "I don't think so," she stuttered. "You're better off bringing your research here."

"You know, Cassie," Adam said. "Now that the protection spell is broken, and Scarlett is getting closer, I think it's time we looped in the rest of the Circle."

Cassie shook her head before he could say anything more. "We've already discussed this. I told you, I need some time before I tell the Circle I have the book. I'm not going to say it again."

"This is some really dark stuff, Cassie." Adam pointed at the text's ominous squiggly lines. "Look at it. Decoding this is going to require as many of us working on it as possible. I think it's worth a shot."

"Oh, is that what you think? You think it's worth a shot?" Cassie realized she was shouting, but she couldn't stop herself. "Well, here's what I think," she said. "I think it's my book, not yours. And it's my issue to deal with, not the Circle's."

"You don't have to yell at me," Adam said calmly.

"Sometimes it's the only way to get you to listen!"

Adam leaned backward. "We're dealing with dark magic here, Cassie. A curse of Black John's that can save the lives of our friends who are marked, not to mention our Circle—but only if we translate it properly."

"Exactly. The book is dangerous, Adam. I don't want anyone to get hurt until I know I have something real that could help them. But if you're so interested in dabbling in dark magic all of a sudden, maybe you should go find Scarlett."

Adam looked stunned. Cassie was, too. She had thought she was feeling better after Adam's romantic gesture before their meeting. She hadn't realized last night's conversation about the cord and Scarlett was still prodding at her heart. But it made her insides ache—even more now that she and Adam were disagreeing—and out it had come before she even knew what she was saying.

"That's not what I meant at all." Adam's voice cracked with emotion, but he strived to maintain his composure. "How could you even think such a thing? You're the one who said it was going to be okay last night. You said, 'Everything will look brighter tomorrow.' Well, that day is today, Cassie, and I'm still here, loving you."

Cassie knew Adam was right. She had tried to assure him Scarlett wouldn't come between them, and now she was ruining that effort. The heated anger within her was driving him away—she knew she should stop, but it felt like her emotions were beyond her control.

What Cassie did next surprised them both. She grabbed Adam's face with her hands and brought his mouth to hers. She kissed him violently, like the life of their relationship depended on it—and maybe it did. Cassie climbed on top of Adam, and he resisted her at first, but as Cassie knew he would, he eventually gave in.

It had never been this way before. Fast, animalistic. Pulling Adam closer always felt good, but right now everything seemed blurry and confused. Cassie's intentions were clouded.

Once they slowed down, Adam drew back and looked into her eyes with concern. "Does this mean we're okay?"

"I don't want to lose you," Cassie said. Her own voice sounded foreign to her, almost anesthetized.

"You're not going to lose me." Adam began kissing her again, but this time Cassie drew back.

She regretted the way she'd yelled at Adam and wanted to react to him with warmth now, but she was oddly disconnected. She wasn't really sure what she was feeling—or if she was feeling anything at all. All she was certain of was that she didn't want to say or do anything else that might hurt him.

Cassie sat up and brought her knees in toward her chest. "I'm sorry," she said. "But I'm just not myself right now. I think you should go."

Adam's face crumpled, a combination of disappointment and confusion, but he simply nodded and got up to gather his things.

"Okay," he said. He glanced down at Black John's book still open on the floor but thought better of mentioning it. "When you're feeling better, I'll be waiting for your call."

He left, quietly shutting Cassie's bedroom door behind him.

The second Cassie heard Adam leave the house, she leapt out of bed. Her father's book was still splayed open on the floor, held in place by the obsidian crystal. Suddenly it all became clear. Her charge of emotions with Adam just now—she'd felt it before. It was the same surge she felt when she handled her father's Book of Shadows.

She got down on her hands and knees and examined the book at eye level. Her fingers trembled with anticipation, still warm from where she'd been singed earlier. The book had some power over her—she understood that now. Each time it burned her hands it affected her mind. It was changing her.

Cassie thought back to every time she'd lost her temper since she'd first opened the book, every disagreement with the Circle, every frustration with her mother. She'd handled the book just before each time. And what had just happened with Adam . . . Cassie had felt how destructive she was being in the moment, but hadn't been able to stop herself. Cassie reached for the book with both hands and the obsidian crystal slid out of place and onto the floor. _The book is the problem_, Cassie thought, _but also the solution_. She flipped through its pages in search of any symbols that struck her as familiar. Minutes passed before she realized she was holding the book without being burned.

Cassie lifted her fingertips up to her eyes. They were perfectly fine. No new marks, no tingling. It was what she'd been hoping for since she'd first taken the book from the basement. But deep down, she couldn't ignore the dismal reason the book no longer rejected her hands. As she was turning darker, it was beginning to welcome her. The balance in Cassie was shifting.

But she couldn't let that scare her. Now that she'd come this far, abandoning her search for the witch-hunter curse wasn't a choice. The threat the book posed would just have to be considered an occupational hazard, a risk that came with the job of saving her Circle.

She continued turning the pages, gaining momentum with every word, absorbing all she could from each dot and stroke. The book's contents still appeared as an archaic code, and she didn't understand most of what she took in, yet there were certain symbols she found especially curious, ciphers that seemed to reach out and speak to her. Cassie could feel the meanings of these lines like a bar of classical music; they moved her from the inside out.

Part of her wanted to run and tell Adam immediately, to show him how peacefully the book lay in her hands.

But if touching the book was changing her, she didn't want anyone else to fall victim to its curse. And she also shouldn't handle the book more than she had to. Or as much as she *wanted* to.

Cassie thought for a moment about her options. She turned back to the book's first page and carried it over to her desk. She pulled out a spiralbound notebook and took a ballpoint pen in hand. She sat and carefully copied the page, line for line, into her notebook, and then she copied the second page as well. It took nearly an hour to painstakingly duplicate every sign and symbol until she had an exact replica, one that could be translated without any doubt. When she was done, she admired the finished product. Cassie would show it to Adam in the morning and apologize to him for her weird behavior. It wouldn't solve all their problems, but it was a good start.

CHAPTER 11

Normally Cassie would have called Adam before showing up at his house first thing in the morning, but she was too anxious to bother with that today. Adam answered his door wearing only striped pajama bottoms. He was surprised to see her, but he appeared pleased as he crossed his arms over his chest in embarrassment and invited her in.

Adam pulled out a kitchen chair for her. There was a half-eaten bowl of cereal on the table—she'd obviously caught him in the middle of breakfast.

"I hope you don't mind me barging in on you like this," Cassie said. "I wanted to say that I'm sorry about my behavior last night."

Adam's posture softened at her apology. "It's okay. We're all under a lot of stress, and emotions are running high."

"It's still no excuse for what I said about Scarlett."

Adam turned away and Cassie felt vaguely uncomfortable. She couldn't tell what he was thinking.

"I brought you something." Cassie reached into her bag to pull out the pages she had transcribed. "I copied the first two pages of my father's book for you."

Adam took the papers and set them down flat on the kitchen table. "You copied these exactly?"

He quietly inspected each line, taking long enough that Cassie began to worry, but before he could say anything negative, she reached out to run her fingers through his unkempt hair.

"You know I can't do this research without you," she said. "That's why I want you to have your own copy."

Adam warmed to her touch. "Thank you for trusting me," he said.

She wished she could be totally honest with him and tell him the book no longer burned her hands, but Adam wouldn't view her ability to handle the book as a necessary evil like she did. He would be too concerned for her safety. Cassie was confident that if dark magic was allowing her to read the book, then she must be stronger now, strong enough to control it.

Adam was silent for a moment, and then he gave Cassie's arm a light stroke. It was a small gesture, but it brought a murmur of release to her lips.

"Just to be extra cautious," he said, "I want you to leave the book alone until I can get to work translating these pages. Can you do that?"

"Of course," Cassie replied, hoping more than anything that she could.

———

The smell of garlic filled Cassie's nose when she arrived home for dinner. Her mom was in the kitchen stirring a pot with a wooden spoon.

"Let me guess," Cassie said as she hung up her jacket. "Italian?"

"Spaghetti and meatballs," her mother said, from over the stove.

Cassie noticed a new energy in her mother's voice and a freshness to her face. Maybe it was having three more kids to keep an eye on that had given her a renewed sense of purpose. Not that Faye, Laurel, and Nick weren't a handful, but it was clear her mother enjoyed having them around the house and playing a role in protecting them from the hunters, and she was flattered they hung around the secret room even more than they had to.

Cassie gave her mother a kiss on the cheek.

"What was that for?"

"Can't I kiss my own mom without having a reason?" Cassie said.

"Of course you can. You just never do." Her mother grinned and handed Cassie an onion and a knife. "But since you love me so much tonight, you can be my sous-chef."

Cassie put on an apron and began chopping while her mother asked her questions about what was going on with her friends and at school. For a moment, Cassie feared her mother's interrogation was trying to get her to admit she'd taken Black John's book from the secret room, but as their small talk progressed, she realized her mother had no idea the book was missing. Cassie told her about what had happened at the dance and about the protection spell being broken. She told her about Diana agreeing to spend more time with Max in spite of the risk it posed. And then she thought about Adam. So much was happening with him, Cassie hardly knew where to begin.

"Scarlett is getting closer," Cassie said. "And I'm a

little worried she could be after more in my life than just my Circle, if you catch my drift."

"You don't mean Adam, do you?"

Cassie nodded and her mother shook her head sympathetically. "Cassie, I'm sorry. I've been through that and I know how it can turn your whole world upside down."

This was the first time Cassie's mom had ever alluded to what had happened with Black John and Scarlett's mother. Cassie made no reaction, hoping her mother would say more.

"And when it's not a Circle member," her mother continued, "but someone close enough to the Circle, that's even worse. Outsiders are always the most difficult to deal with."

Cassie wiped a few onion tears from her eyes with her forearm. Did that mean Scarlett's mother hadn't been a Circle member? Cassie had always assumed she was.

"The tensions that kind of thing can cause within a Circle can be brutal," her mother said. "No matter how strong that Circle is. Our Circle was strong, but it still tore us all apart."

Then she put down her wooden spoon and her face became tender. "I'm sorry," she said. "Pay no attention to me when I carry on like that. It's just that sometimes old hurts are hard to shake."

"It's okay," Cassie said. "It's good for me to hear it. I can handle it."

"I know you can, honey. But that doesn't mean you should have to deal with my jaded past. My experiences aren't yours, and they don't have to be."

Her mother rested her hands on Cassie's shoulders. "Adam is a good boy," she said. "He's worth fighting for."

"But what if I lose?" Cassie asked.

Her mother looked at her lovingly. "All that's in your power is to try. The outcome will be what it'll be. But ultimately, Cassie, the people who are meant to be together will end up together."

In spite of all the heartbreak her mother had endured, Cassie could see she truly believed those words. But her mother had ended up alone after all. And Scarlett's mother had ended up dead. Cassie wasn't sure if her mother's indestructible faith inspired her or filled her with sadness.

"So don't you worry," her mother said. "You just focus on figuring out what to do with your father's book—figure out how to break that spell so you can open it safely, without getting burned. The rest will all fall into place."

Cassie felt a twinge of guilt for not telling her mother that she'd already been studying the book. But she couldn't bring herself to confess. There still had to be some secrets, even between them.

Her mom was right about one thing, though: The book was the only thing capable of getting Cassie out of this mess.

CHAPTER 12

Cassie arrived at the beach for the full moon ceremony just as Diana was drawing a circle in the sand with her pearl-handled knife. It was already five minutes to midnight, when the moon would be at its highest point, so she had to hurry.

Diana went around the circle with water she'd collected from the ocean, then with a stick of calamus-scented incense, and finally with a lighted white candle. Pungent, smoky smells filled the air.

"Cassie," Adam called out when he spotted her. "Where've you been? I've been calling you."

"I'm sorry. I know." Cassie continued watching Diana.

"I was helping my mom clean up after dinner and I lost track of time."

"Uh-oh," Faye said, loud enough for everyone to hear. "Don't you two know good communication is the foundation of a healthy relationship?"

"Actually," Suzan said, "I'm pretty sure it's trust."

Faye smirked. "No, that can't be it."

Adam was not amused by their banter. "I had something important to tell you." He made an effort to pull Cassie aside. "That's why I kept calling."

"You guys! It's almost midnight, come on!" Diana held a lit candle in one hand and reached out to grab Cassie with the other. But she clutched Cassie's pointer and index fingers just where her most recent burns had scabbed over. Cassie cried out softly in pain.

Diana looked at her, confused. "Are you okay?"

Cassie stretched the sleeves of her shirt down over her hands.

"Did I hurt you?" Diana asked.

Faye and the others gathered around Cassie. "Lift up your sleeves," Faye commanded.

After a glance at Adam, Cassie did as she was told.

Immediately, everyone's eyes settled on the scars and scabs she'd been working so hard to keep hidden.

Cassie looked around and realized the time had come for her to tell them about her father's book. There was no other way of explaining the burns, and Cassie didn't want to outright lie to her Circle—they didn't deserve that.

With an encouraging nod from Adam, and with the group's rapt attention, Cassie made a clear, concise announcement: "I have Black John's Book of Shadows," she said. "It's what gave me these scars."

"You found—you mean—are you serious?" Diana sputtered.

Cassie nodded. "I've been searching it for any hint on how to defeat the hunters or Scarlett. But it's dangerous," Cassie continued, holding up her hands as an example. "You have to understand, I don't want anyone else to get hurt, not until I know it can help us."

Faye leaned on Sean to keep from falling over. "Black John's book has been in your house this whole time? And you kept it from me?" She was practically hyper-ventilating. "I can't even imagine the spells that must be in there. Go get it, Cassie. Right now."

Cassie shook her head. "I can't read it, and neither can you. It's written in an ancient language. And besides, we don't know what the book is capable of."

"Actually, Cassie," Adam interrupted, "that's why I kept calling you earlier."

Seagulls squawked in circles overhead as Adam regarded the group, a gloomy look on his face. "Cassie showed me a portion of the book yesterday, and I was up all night trying to translate it. I compared some of the symbols in the book to the ancient map I used to locate the Master Tools."

Diana nodded, knowing that map well. "I remember those inscriptions," she said. "Black John had written them himself."

Adam fixed his eyes on Cassie again. His voice was a stricken monotone. "From the little bits and pieces I could figure out, Cassie is now bound to Black John's book."

For a few seconds Cassie lost her hearing. The hammering thump of her heartbeat was the only sound in her ears. She could see everyone's reactions—Diana's terror, Faye's apprehension, Adam's distress—but she felt like she was watching them from somewhere hushed and far away. It was gruesome, the way the faces of her friends altered. Not one of them would ever think of Cassie the same way again.

"Are you sure?" Diana asked. Her voice hit Cassie's ears with a *pop*.

"*Bound* was definitely the word I translated," Adam said. "And any dark magic involving that word can't be good."

Diana took a deep breath. "No. Not good at all."

"What exactly does this mean?" Suzan asked.

"In the scientific sense," Laurel said, "being bound simply means being held to another element. It's a union, physical or chemical. And it's inseparable."

Melanie cut in to clarify. "Simply put, it means Cassie's obligated to the book. As in *tied in bonds*. Like a prisoner."

"Melanie." Diana chastised her with a glare. "It's an attachment. That's all. Don't jump to worst-case scenarios."

Cassie wanted the group to believe Diana was right: that being bound to the book only meant she was attached to it, nothing more. But Cassie couldn't deny what she knew to be the truth: The book did have an influence over her. Every time she touched it, it was like darkness took her over. She was beginning to feel like she had a split personality.

Cassie began to cry, and Adam walked slowly over to her. He put his arm around her torso. "Cassie, I'm sorry you're going through all this. But the Circle can help you now. You're not in this alone."

"That's right." Diana took a step closer and also put her arm around Cassie. "We can all look into those symbols and help with the translation."

"You can copy a few pages at a time for us to study," Adam said. "Using the obsidian crystal, so you're as safe as possible."

There were supportive nods around the Circle, except from Faye who crossed her arms over her chest. "Just to be clear," she said. "We are talking about Cassie being undeniably linked to dark magic, right? That's what Black John's book is, and that's what Cassie's bound to."

A heartrending stillness settled over the group like a heavy quilt. There was absolute silence except for the roar and crashing of waves in the distance.

Adam nodded grimly. "Like Scarlett, Cassie does have dark magic in her blood, and the book is obviously reacting to that." He turned to Cassie and swallowed hard. "In fact, as someone who knows dark magic so well, Scarlett might be able to tell us something useful about the book. Maybe she can help."

Cassie stared down at the sand, unable to speak.

"Adam," Nick shouted. "You do remember that Scarlett is out to kill your girlfriend, right?"

Faye raised an eyebrow. "Trading off Princess Cassie

for Evil Witch Scarlett? That sounds like a great suggestion to me."

"And while we're at it, we can get the Master Tools back," Deborah said.

"That's not what I meant." Adam shot Cassie a desperate look. "I just meant we could confront her. Maybe even bargain with her."

"No way," Nick said. "If we find Scarlett, we're taking her down, not asking her for advice."

Cassie forced down the bile that had risen in her throat. She staggered back to the center of the group and everyone got quiet again, their faces turned toward her expectantly.

"It's not a bad idea to try to get information out of Scarlett." She looked at Adam with a strained smile, though she was beginning to wonder if he had feelings for Scarlett he wasn't admitting—even to himself. "But we're dealing with two evils here, and at least the book can't fight back." And with that, Cassie had the final word.

CHAPTER 13

Cassie was nodding off in eighth-period math to the drone of Mr. Zitofsky explaining the quadratic equation when she heard the unmistakable buzz of her phone vibrating in her bag. It was a text message from Diana:

COME TO THE BAND ROOM. NOW. EMERGENCY MEETING.

Cassie looked across the room at Melanie, who had clearly gotten the same text message. They exchanged a worried glace as Melanie started gathering her things. The Circle had spent the last week translating Black John's book in bits and pieces from the pages Cassie had copied; maybe someone had stumbled onto something important.

Cassie preferred that theory to the alternative: that something terrible had happened.

But how would Cassie and Melanie escape from the classroom now without drawing suspicion?

As if someone had read her mind, the fire alarm went off. Mr. Zitofsky took off his glasses and rose from his seat. "Okay, everyone," he said. "You know the drill. Up and out, single file."

Another text, this time from Nick, confirmed Cassie's suspicions:

FALSE ALARM. YOU'RE WELCOME. BAND ROOM, NOW.

Cassie fought the urge to grin as she and Melanie followed her classmates, soldierlike, out the door. The crowded hallways teeming with students striding toward the emergency exits made sneaking away to the band room easy. They let themselves in just as Chris asked, "What are we doing in here?" Then he picked up a French horn and blew into it with all his might.

"It was the only empty room we could find that also happens to be soundproofed," Deborah said. And then she looked at Cassie. "Glad you could make it."

Everyone from the Circle except Adam was already gathered in the dimly lit room the band kids called the

Pit. But only Chris and Doug fiddled with the assorted brass instruments strewn about.

Adam stepped in the door and Nick said, "That's everyone. Now what's going on?"

Chris and Doug set down their clarinets and waited, along with the rest of the group, for Diana to say something. Cassie got the sense this announcement had nothing to do with the book. Diana had been trailing Max quite a bit, spending more and more time alone with him this past week, and Cassie had an awful feeling her announcement had something to do with him.

Diana stepped to the center of the floor and stood in front of an empty music stand. "I have disheartening news," she said.

"We're shocked," Faye called out.

"Do we ever have emergency *good news* meetings?" Deborah added.

Diana took something out of her back pocket. "I found this today when I was going through Max's bag."

Faye mumbled under her breath, "You've been spending enough time together, it's about time you found something useful on him."

"Excuse me?" Diana said. "Do you have something you'd like to say to me?"

Faye shook her head. "No. Nothing. Just wondering what you found."

Diana walked solemnly over to Suzan and Deborah. "It's a picture," she said. "Of the two of you."

Deborah took the photograph from Diana's hand and stared at it. Suzan looked at it over her shoulder.

Cassie watched Deborah's face turn from pink, to red, to light purple. Then she crumpled the picture in her fist and threw it violently onto the floor.

Cassie bent down to pick it up, smoothing it out to view its image. It was a photograph of Suzan and Deborah on the night of the Spring Fling. It looked like it had been taken from far away, maybe on a cell phone—it had a grainy surveillance look to it. It was from after the power had gone out, and it looked like Deborah and Suzan had used magic to light their way in the dark. But the most disturbing part was that over Suzan's and Deborah's faces, the photo was stamped with the mark of the hunter.

Cassie turned the photo around so the whole Circle could see it. "Now almost half of us are marked," she said.

"How did this happen?" Melanie asked, examining the photograph. "This was taken the night of the dance. How did we not know about this until now?"

Suzan nodded soberly. "We knew we'd been marked.

We just . . . we didn't want to tell you all just yet. It was stupid of us."

"The secret is out now." Deborah retreated to the corner. She pounded the wall with her fist, and Cassie worried that she might have punched right through the plaster.

It *was* stupid of them—to use magic in the first place, and to not tell the Circle they'd been caught—but nobody had the heart to criticize them for their poor judgment. Not when they were facing far graver consequences.

"This has gone way too far." Adam stood up. "Two more members being marked means we have to take action."

"We've made some progress translating the book," Laurel offered. "The pages we worked on yesterday could be the witch-hunter curse we've been looking for."

Diana shook her head. "But it's a haphazard translation. It's nowhere near ready yet."

"I'd say giving it a try is long overdue." Faye went over to where Deborah was hovering in the corner and led her back to the group. "Let's go get our revenge."

But Diana stood her ground in spite of the circumstances. "We don't want to use dark magic we don't understand. It's too dangerous."

"Then it's time we go after Scarlett." Faye was growing

frustrated. She leaned forward with her jaw set and her golden eyes gleaming. "She's the only one who can help us understand dark magic."

Adam sensibly kept quiet on the matter this time, but Diana surprised everyone by speaking up. "I agree," she said, and then she looked at Cassie regretfully. "It's time."

"We're not strong enough to overpower Scarlett, remember?" Melanie said. "Not even all of us put together."

Diana took a chance and put her arm around Cassie. "We're strong enough if we get the Master Tools back."

Cassie raised her eyes just in time to see Adam smile. "Exactly," he said. "With the Tools, we were strong enough to defeat Black John himself."

"Then I guess we have to find Scarlett," Nick said. "But just to get the Tools back. That's all we can risk right now."

Everyone seemed to be in agreement—even Nick. But all Cassie could think about was her mother telling her that if she had any chance of defeating Scarlett, the answers were in the book. Nothing seemed possible or realistic anymore without the secrets it contained.

"Cassie," Diana said, and only then did Cassie realize the whole group was watching her. "We need you with us on this."

Cassie looked at each of them. Diana appeared desperate but sincere. Deborah and Suzan were newly terrified. Faye was out for blood. Finally, Cassie rested her eyes on Adam. He appeared repentant and regretful for bringing Scarlett back to the forefront of their lives. But he was doing what he thought was best for her, and for their friends. That was plain to see.

The whole Circle really believed they could do it. They thought they could triumph over evil without resorting to darkness. Cassie envied them, really. There was a time she had believed that was possible, too.

But what could she say? They were her Circle, and she was obligated to go down with them, if that's what they were going to do.

"I'm with you," she said. "Let's go get our Tools back."

CHAPTER 14

That night Diana and Adam gathered salt water from the rising tide, while Cassie and the others prepared the secret room for a locator spell to find Scarlett. Suzan and Deborah set up candles on all four cardinal points: north, south, east, and west. Sean lit their wicks one at a time. Chris and Doug cleansed the air with smoking jasmine censers, while Melanie laid out energy-clearing crystals. Cassie allowed a small part of herself to fill with hope. Maybe they did have enough good magic behind them to stand a chance in this fight. Getting the Master Tools back from Scarlett could change everything.

Diana and Adam returned from outside with a stone cauldron filled to the brim with seawater. They set it down on the floor, and the group joined hands around it, enclosing it in a circle. Just as they had the last time the Circle performed this spell, they all concentrated on the water—on its clarity and depth, its ability to reshape its form to any container, and its utility as a mirror. Then they invoked the elements.

"Power of water, I beseech you," Diana said. Together the Circle softly repeated the locator chant four times:

She who is lost shall now be found
Hiding places come unbound

They stared into the cauldron as Diana called out, "Let the water show the location of Scarlett."

Then they watched, waiting for the images to come.

Cassie focused hard, directing all her yearning and desire onto the water. She bent her mind, begging it to cooperate. When the first image started to form she felt a gust of energy rush through her.

It was an old house—seventeenth-century old. And it was surrounded by a heavy iron gate. The house looked like it should have been a museum, no longer suitable to live in, but not unlike many houses in New Salem and on the mainland.

Then Cassie saw a bridge, but not one she recognized. It could have been any bridge anywhere; nothing about it struck her as unique. It disappeared as quickly as it had appeared.

Finally a strange picture began coming together on the surface of the water. Bit by bit, a startling portrait came to light: a man with his head and feet locked through holes in a wooden board. His hands were chained behind him. Cassie knew what she was looking at—she'd seen one of these before. It was a prisoner in colonial-era stocks. Then the water turned to a disquieting black.

Cassie wasn't sure what to make of the strange series of images. It seemed like the spell hadn't worked nearly as well as it had the last time. But Adam looked up at the others with understanding in his eyes. "I can't believe it," he said. "She's so close to New Salem."

"I know that place." Nick nodded along. "It's the old Stockbridge Mission House, just on the other side of the bridge. It's supposed to be abandoned, but I guess it's not anymore."

"Well, what are we waiting for?" Faye asked. "Let's go get her."

"Hold on." Diana blew out all the candles and snuffed out the incense. "First we should research what spells would be useful against Scarlett. So we're at least prepared for a face-off."

Laurel pulled out a notebook and began jotting down a list. "We should study our defense spells," she said. "And definitely remote summoning spells. Melanie, can you look into what crystals might be of use?"

Faye flicked Laurel's pencil from her fingers. "Forget all that. We've got Cassie."

Cassie looked down at the tattered throw rug, not wanting to acknowledge Faye's comment. Of course Faye was champing at the bit to attack the hunters. All she cared about was breaking her mark, even if it meant Cassie performing dark magic. But what Faye didn't understand was the more Cassie used dark magic, the darker she became. Or maybe Faye did understand that, but she was still willing to sacrifice Cassie to the dark side for their cause.

"Cassie's not using black magic when we go up against Scarlett," Adam said. "Under any circumstances. But aside from that, I agree with Faye. We need to act right away, even if we don't have all the research."

Diana gawked at Adam from across the living room table. "This isn't something to rush into," she said. "Need

I remind you how in our last battle with Scarlett, she made you blind with a single wave of her hand?"

Suzan and Deborah, who were sitting side by side on the sofa, chuckled meanly.

"I remember," Adam said. "And it wasn't just me, it was all of us. But thanks for bringing that up."

Adam turned to Nick for support, assuming they might for once fall on the same side of a dispute. "Don't you think it's do-or-die time?" Adam said to Nick. "Study period is over. Am I right?"

Cassie's insides were seething. She wanted to go after Scarlett and get the Master Tools back more than any of them, but deep down she knew what they were up against—she was the *only* one who really understood what they were up against. It was her responsibility to speak up.

"Having learned something from the trap I walked into in Cape Cod," she said, "I don't want to face Scarlett unprepared. She's stronger than all of us put together. We got lucky last time—we got her to run away, but we couldn't overpower her. The only way we stand a chance of defeating her now is by outsmarting her."

Cassie directed her attention to Adam. "That was a great pep talk and all, but a positive attitude and a whole lot of hope aren't going to cut it. We need to be realistic.

We should have an arsenal of spells at our fingertips before we step through the door of that house. One or two more days of preparation is all we need. It's not much."

"I'm with her," Deborah said. "Cassie should be the one calling the shots on this mission."

Nick raised his hand. "I second that."

Adam's cheeks turned crimson, and Faye let out a begrudging sigh.

Laurel picked up her notebook and pencil. "Okay then. Who has something to add to the list?"

~~~~~~~~~~~~

Adam lingered at Cassie's front door, waiting for the others to leave her house with their individual assignments. He tilted his head at her and averted his eyes. "We should talk," he said.

"About what?"

"Scarlett."

"It seems like she's *all* you want to talk about lately," Cassie said.

Adam's coy look changed into something more serious. "I understand why you're upset, Cassie. But I didn't suggest we find Scarlett so I could ask her out to dinner." He smiled. "You know that."

Cassie did know that, but she still resented Scarlett for

the stress she was putting on her and Adam's relationship. And that resentment was transferring directly onto Adam.

"That's all I wanted to say." Adam leaned in and gave Cassie a stiff hug good-bye.

Cassie accepted his hug with limp arms. In her mind, she knew Adam hadn't done anything wrong, but her heart was proving to be more stubborn. Scarlett and the cord were all she could see when she looked at Adam now, all she could feel when he touched her. No matter how hard she tried to rationalize her jealousy away, it was there.

After Adam left, Cassie did the only thing she could think of to distract herself from her love life: She started cleaning the kitchen. Her mother would be home soon, and it would be nice for her to return to a spotless house.

As she was sweeping the kitchen floor, enjoying the trivial sense of control that came from defeating household dirt and grime, Nick climbed up from the basement.

Cassie gripped her broom handle tightly. "Going somewhere?" she asked.

Nick slipped the broom out of Cassie's hands. "Not unless you're volunteering yourself as an escort."

"I might be." Cassie laughed. "But not until this floor is clean."

"In that case, consider it done." Nick put his head

down and began sweeping the floor with even strokes.

Cassie watched him, admiring the way he could lose himself so effortlessly in a physical task. Rebuilding engines, wrenching pipes, chopping wood—brute force was where Nick excelled. Fixing things that were broken, or muscling a floor clean if that was all he could get. There was a rugged simplicity to him that Cassie envied.

Nick stopped sweeping and rested both hands on the broom handle. "A penny for your thoughts," he said.

"I should be the one paying you if I start talking."

"Try me." Nick grinned. "First session is free."

Cassie leaned against the kitchen counter. "Well, for starters, I've been having terrible nightmares."

"From the book, do you think?" Nick asked.

"I guess. I've been having a lot of weird feelings since that book came into my life." Cassie paused. "And things with Adam have gotten pretty messy."

Nick usually flinched every time Cassie said Adam's name, but he didn't this time. His mahogany eyes were still and clear and his face was calm. Cassie suddenly felt like she could tell Nick anything and he wouldn't judge her. She took a step closer to him.

"You know the cord?" she asked. "The one between me and Adam?"

"The infamous silver cord. Do you even have to ask?"

"Well, there's another one just like it," Cassie said. "Between Adam and Scarlett."

"Hmm." Nick set the broom aside and crossed his thick arms over his chest.

"What do you think that means?" Cassie asked.

"The more important question is what do *you* think it means?" Nick's voice was caring and warm.

Cassie shook her head. "I'm not sure."

"Personally," Nick said. He looked pointedly at Cassie. "I think people pick who they love."

There was a beat of silence between them, a charged moment, and Cassie felt something tremble inside her. Something uncontrollable. A heat.

Without thinking, she took Nick's face into her hands and kissed him. It was urgent, and passionate, nothing like her soft kisses with Adam. She was hungry in a way she didn't know she was capable of. But at the same time she felt disconnected, the way she had felt in her bedroom that night with Adam, after touching the book. It was like her mind and her body had split. She wanted to stop, but she couldn't, so she kept kissing Nick until he pulled away.

He brought his fingers to his lips in shock. "What the heck was that?"

Cassie was just as stunned as he was. "I don't know," she said. "I'm sorry."

"Don't do that unless you mean it." Nick's eyes blazed at her, and the air between them still felt charged. Cassie knew if she didn't walk away now she was going to do something she might really regret. She turned and ran up the stairs to her bedroom, securing the door behind her.

Cassie wasn't sure what to make of what had just happened. She hadn't known she was going to kiss Nick until she was already kissing him. In the moment, the thrill of it had rushed through her whole body. The screaming black hunger from deep in her gut was satiated—it had gotten what it wanted—but now all Cassie felt was empty.

CHAPTER 15

The next morning, guilt and shame were consuming Cassie from the inside out. It was only a kiss, but it shouldn't have happened. How could she have let it happen? Before she even kicked off the covers and got out of bed she tried calling Adam. She had to set things right.

He answered right away but sounded distracted. Or was he annoyed?

"Is this a bad time?" Cassie asked.

"It's fine," Adam said abruptly. "What's up?"

"I was hoping we could talk," Cassie said. "Will you meet me out on the bluff?"

"I can't."

"It's kind of important."

Adam nervously cleared his throat. "I wish I could, but I have to study for a history test."

He was so obviously lying that it was almost insulting. "Since when are you so concerned about studying?" Cassie said.

"What are you talking about? Since always."

Cassie knew something was wrong. Adam's voice sounded agitated and higher-pitched than usual. He was hiding something.

"Can I talk to you now then, for a few minutes?" Cassie asked. "There's something I'd like to say and I don't want to put it off."

"You know, now really isn't such a good time. I'm kind of in the middle of something."

Cassie could hardly believe her ears. Adam must be angry with her or he would never behave this way. But it didn't make sense. Just last night he had told her he loved her.

"I really do want to talk," Adam said. "But it'll have to wait. I'm sorry, Cassie, but I've got to go. I'll call you later."

Cassie said good-bye and then listened to the silence on Adam's end of the line for a few seconds after he hung up. The rift between them must be bigger than she had thought. And Adam didn't even know the worst of it yet.

If he was this upset with her now, what would his reaction be when he found out she had kissed Nick?

Hours passed, and Cassie still couldn't get the phone call with Adam out of her head. It wasn't only the fact that he had lied that was upsetting her. It was that she deserved it. He was right to not even want to hear her pathetic apology. If she were him, she wouldn't want to talk to her either.

But there was someone else Cassie should apologize to, and she hoped he would at least hear her out. She filled up a few plates with some chicken and vegetables and brought them downstairs, just as an excuse to seek out Nick.

When she stepped inside the secret room, Nick was hunkered on the couch watching a bad horror movie with Deborah and Suzan. They were munching on popcorn and laughing. None of them turned to look at her, but the moment Cassie laid eyes on Nick she was overcome with shame. She couldn't even bear the sight of him. She set the food she'd brought on the kitchen table and turned to run back upstairs as fast as she could.

Nick noticed her and bolted up to catch her by the arm. "Hey," he said. "Where are you going?"

Cassie glanced at Faye and Laurel, but neither of them noticed the commotion. They were both at their computers wearing headphones. And Deborah and Suzan were too engrossed in the blood and guts of their movie to care about what Nick and Cassie had going on. They turned up the volume on the TV to drown their voices out.

Nick pulled Cassie aside. "You're avoiding me. There's no reason for that. If we have to talk about it, we should talk about it."

Cassie's mind began swimming too fast to complete a coherent sentence. "I don't know what happened last night," she said. "I'm sorry, I haven't been myself lately."

"Take it easy," Nick said. "Nothing catastrophic happened."

"Nick, I kissed you. I practically jumped your bones. Adam would think it was pretty catastrophic."

Nick smirked. "True. But I kind of understand why it happened."

"I wish I understood. I've been working so hard to get you to be my friend again, and then I go and . . ." Cassie couldn't finish the sentence.

"Look, it was just a fleeting moment," Nick said dismissively. "I've had a million moments where I wanted to do something like that."

"You have?" Cassie took a deep breath. "I don't want this to mean—"

"It doesn't mean we should be anything more again," Nick said. "Or that you should jeopardize what you have with Adam. I get that."

This cool reaction from Nick didn't exactly match their heated exchange yesterday, but Cassie would take what she could get. "You forgive me then," she said.

Nick shook his head. "Stuff happens sometimes, Cassie. Especially between good friends. Wires get crossed; things get confused."

"So that's what we are?" Cassie asked. "Good friends? Still?"

Nick avoided the question by glancing at the movie he was missing. "Although it was a pretty hot kiss, if I do say so myself." He smiled, and Cassie tried to ignore the slightly condescending note in his voice.

The fact was, she was lucky enough to have not one but *two* guys in her life who really cared about her. If only she felt worthy of either of them right now.

She thought back to her tense conversation with Adam. If they were drifting apart, she wasn't going to let their relationship end without a fight. Refusing to let Scarlett, or Nick, or anyone get between them was the only way to prove to Adam that she loved him—and proving it was more important now than ever.

"I'm glad we've cleared the air," Cassie said. "Now I should probably go do damage control with my boyfriend."

"I guess that means you're going to tell him," Nick said.

"I have to. I know it won't help your friendship, but I can't keep it from him."

"Maybe you should remind him that this room is spelled for protection. So he'll have to drag me out of it if he wants to kill me."

"Let's hope it won't come to that. Besides, I think this time I'll be the one taking the blame." Cassie gave Nick a peck on the cheek. "Wish me luck."

"You don't need luck," Nick said. "Adam's not going to let you go that easily."

Cassie ran back upstairs and out of the house, sprinting down the sun-drenched block while practicing her apology to Adam in her head. She found herself at the wooden threshold of his front door within minutes. Adam's Mustang, she noticed, was absent from the driveway, but he often parked it inside the garage, so that didn't mean much. First Cassie knocked on the heavy oak door, and then she rang the bell. But all she could hear on the other side was Raj's incessant barking. Adam wasn't home.

Nobody was, it seemed. But ever since their conversation that morning, Cassie had known something was off. She suddenly imagined Adam hiding inside, waiting for her to give up and leave him alone.

Would he really pretend to not be home?

Cassie looked to her left and right; there was no one in sight except for a blue uniformed mailman wearing giant headphones and bobbing to music only he could hear. Cassie hastily used a spell to unlock the door. It unlatched with a click, and she squeaked it open. Inside Raj was jumping and barking anxiously, as if he knew something was wrong. She gave the dog a pat to quiet him and scanned the shadowy living room and den.

Where could Adam be? Wherever he was, he clearly didn't want her to know, or he wouldn't have sounded so strange on the phone earlier.

Cassie crept into Adam's bedroom to have a quick look around. His bed was an unmade mountain of blankets, and his history books were lying unopened on his nightstand. He obviously wasn't studying for a history test. At least now she had proof he'd been lying.

She searched his desk for some clue as to where he might have gone, or what he was up to. As she shifted a few papers to the side, her finger accidentally brushed against the mouse to his computer and the monitor came to life. A gray image of an old house filled the screen. It was the Stockbridge Mission House, Cassie was sure of it. It was the very same house that had appeared during the locator spell. And below its ghostly image were step-by-step driving directions to get there from New Salem.

He didn't, Cassie thought.

But as she clicked through the information on Adam's computer, it became more and more clear that *he had*. It was the only logical explanation, and it suddenly all made sense—his lies and anxious tone on the phone, and how at their meeting he'd reluctantly agreed to do more research when only a moment before he'd been itching to go after Scarlett immediately. *Do-or-die time*, he'd called it.

Adam had gone after Scarlett. Alone.

CHAPTER 16

How could Adam be so stubborn? And so stupid? He didn't stand a chance against Scarlett by himself. Cassie hurried out of Adam's house in a panic and headed straight to Diana's. Diana would know what to do.

She banged on the glossy front door of Diana's lemon-yellow house, but nobody answered. *Not again,* Cassie thought. She was ready to do another unlocking spell when she tried the nickel handle. It clicked easily beneath her thumb. The door was unlocked. Cassie stepped inside the house's slick foyer and called Diana's name. Her voice echoed off the polished mantel and brass knickknacks.

There was no answer, but the thumping bass of too-loud music echoed from Diana's bedroom. That explained why she hadn't heard Cassie knocking. Cassie made her way up to Diana's room and pushed open her door.

"Diana?" she said, as the image before her registered. Diana wasn't alone. She was on the bed with—

"Oh my God." It was Max. And he was kissing Diana. And she was kissing him back.

"Cassie!" Diana screamed, pulling away from Max hastily. "What are you doing here?"

"The door was open," Cassie stuttered. "I tried knocking, but—I'm sorry."

Max jumped from the bed to a standing position and in one quick motion turned off the music. "It's not what it looks like," he said. He was up on the balls of his feet and his tanned calves were flexed, like he was poised to sidestep the rush of a full-on attack.

"It's okay." Diana looked sympathetically at Max. "It was only a matter of time before someone found us out. At least it's Cassie."

Max settled back on his heels and ran his hands through his hair. Then he dug around on the floor for his socks and sneakers. "You two probably need to talk," he said in a voice that sounded like an apology. "I should go."

"You don't have to leave," Diana said to him, softly. "Just give us a minute."

Cassie stepped aside as Max staggered toward the doorway, avoiding her eyes. "I'll be downstairs." He closed the door behind him, and Cassie turned to Diana.

"Please let me explain," Diana said, without giving Cassie a chance to react.

Cassie didn't know what to say. She needed to tell Diana about Adam going to the Mission House—it was a matter of life and death. But before she could get out even one word, Diana broke into tears.

"This secret has been killing me." Diana's emerald-green eyes grew pink with emotion. "I'm sorry I didn't tell you. I just . . . I knew it would be hard for anyone to understand."

Cassie sat down on the soft-feathered bedspread across from Diana and let her talk. She'd obviously been holding this in for a while and needed to get a lot off her chest.

"When I started spending time with Max," Diana said, "I found myself really liking him. It might not seem like it, Cassie, but he's charming, and sweet. And despite how he sometimes acts in school, he doesn't care what anyone else thinks."

"I don't doubt it." Cassie tried to sound objective and unprejudiced. "But Max is our enemy. He marked Faye himself and his people killed Constance and Portia. He must know you're a witch, too."

Diana nodded, starting to sob. "I know that. I haven't forgotten all that he's done to us. But the cord? The connection that you and Adam have? I've seen that between me and Max."

Cassie swallowed the lump in her throat that formed at the mention of the silver cord. They seemed to be popping up everywhere lately. "Are you sure?" she asked.

Diana was crying so hard, Cassie knew she couldn't be mistaken.

"You of all people must understand," Diana begged. "You can't always choose who you fall for."

Cassie recognized that Diana never would have chosen this path if she'd had a choice. She felt sorry for her in a way. It couldn't be easy, falling in love with your sworn enemy.

Cassie rubbed Diana's back in gentle circles. "I don't blame you for falling for him. He's gorgeous and he's loved you since the first time he saw you. But I guess it's hard for me to understand exactly *how* this happened."

Diana reached for a tissue to wipe her tear-muddled face. "When I was trying to spend time with him, to spy on him, I got to see what it was actually like to *be* him. How he's had to move around from place to place his entire life chasing witches with his awful father. How he has no mom, no siblings. Just like so many of us, Cassie."

Diana plucked a fresh Kleenex from the box and dabbed her eyes. "It's so hard for him to trust people. He's scared and alone. Do you know how that started to feel? To trick this really good guy into believing I had no ulterior motives for spending time with him?"

Diana didn't wait for Cassie to answer. "And then one day we were hanging out in his room and his father came home early. The moment the front door slammed, Max turned to me, terrified. He grabbed my hand and led me to the window and I realized it was me he was worried about, not himself. We climbed out his window and dashed for the woods behind his house. We were barefoot, with our shoes in our hands, and rocks and twigs cut up the bottoms of our muddied feet, but we didn't stop. Long after it was obvious we were safe, Max was still clutching my hand, pulling me along, until finally I couldn't go on. I stopped, breathless, and asked him why we were still running. And that was when he kissed me for the first time. He leaned in and placed his lips on mine, and a wave of energy passed through me like nothing I'd ever felt before. He said, 'I want to keep running until we're free.' And it was as if I were suddenly floating outside myself. I could see the two of us standing there in the woods and how we were connected by a band of energy—a silver cord that hummed and sang and bound us heart to heart. And I understood that it could never be broken, that our lives were linked."

Cassie remained silent, looking at Diana with sympathetic eyes.

"I know it sounds crazy," Diana said, "but I trust him, Cassie. He wouldn't do anything to hurt me."

"If you trust him," Cassie said, "I trust you. But as things progress, it's likely there will be a battle between us and them. You understand that, don't you?"

"I know." Diana exhaled deeply. "It's practically all I can think about. But until we get to that point, can I ask you to keep this between us?"

Cassie wanted to be supportive, but she worried

about the position Diana was now in. She would be torn between her love for Max and her devotion to the Circle, and Cassie knew how powerful the draw of true love could be.

"Let me ask you an important question," Cassie said. "And I need you to tell me the truth. Is there any chance your loyalties will be skewed when it comes time to fight?"

"There is absolutely no chance of that happening." Diana had stopped crying, but her eyes remained puffy and red. "I assure you. My allegiance will always remain with the Circle, even if it kills me. I'm just not ready for them to hear about this yet. Please."

Diana sounded pretty convincing. And she was right that the Circle would never understand how she could possibly be in love with Max.

"Your secret is safe with me," Cassie said. "But we're not done talking about this."

Then Cassie stood up to leave. All this talk about cords and irresistible connections was making her even more nervous about Adam. But she didn't want to risk explaining the Adam situation to Diana with Max so close by.

"Wait." Diana followed Cassie toward the door when

she realized she was leaving. "Didn't you need me for something?"

"Nothing important," Cassie said. "Never mind."

She would have to go after Adam alone. But she had to go now, before it was too late.

CHAPTER 17

*Using the driving directions she had found on Adam's com-*puter, Cassie arrived in Stockbridge just after sunset. The Mission House was hard to miss once she had crossed the bridge. It was an old gray house in terrible disrepair with crooked wooden shutters and moss lurking up its facade—just how it had looked in the water of the location spell.

And just as she saw it in the spell, the house was surrounded by a pointed iron gate. Cassie found it was low enough to pull herself up and over it without difficulty. She landed with both feet upon the spongy mud of the side yard and began exploring the fenced-in property.

Cassie walked the perimeter, figuring out all her

options for entering the house—and also for escape. As far as she could tell, there were three doors—one in front, one at the back, and one on the side of the house. All of them looked shoddy, flimsy, and easy to open, but the back door wasn't even latched closed. It creaked open in the faint breeze.

Cassie let herself inside quietly and then waited for her intuition to alert her to where Adam was. She closed her eyes and centered her energy, calling him with her mind.

But then she heard something in the main room. It was a wispy, delicate sound—the wrinkling bend of pages turning.

Cassie followed it down a long, musty hallway. The sound echoed periodically, guiding her through the dark and across the dusty hardwood floor. It led her right to the threshold of the main room.

It was a carelessly-laid-out space filled with what looked like secondhand furniture. Everything was mismatched, as if the owner had just left all the odds and ends he didn't want in one room before abandoning the place.

Adam was there, standing before Scarlett, breathing heavily. "I brought you your father's Book of Shadows," he said. "What more do you want from me? I have nothing else to offer."

The book. Cassie thought she had recognized its call, and now her worst fear was confirmed. Adam must have taken the book from her room. He was the only one who knew where it was hidden and where to find the key.

The book's worn leather cover looked even more sinister than usual in Scarlett's pale hands, and Cassie's insides stirred. That book was *hers*, just like Adam was hers.

Scarlett leaned in close to Adam, so their faces were nearly touching. "I want from you exactly what you want from me."

Adam didn't turn away. "All I want from you are the Master Tools," he said, his mouth just centimeters from Scarlett's. "Nothing else."

Cassie started to interrupt, to reveal herself, but stopped at the last moment. Adam was safe, for the time being. And in Cape Cod, Scarlett had the upper hand, but Cassie had the element of surprise. If Cassie could catch Scarlett at the right moment . . . her mind started spinning with possibilities.

"You're lying." Scarlett rested her hand on Adam's chest and held it there. "But at least your heartbeat tells the truth."

Adam stepped back, swatting Scarlett's hand from his body. "I know the Tools are here somewhere. If you're not willing to hand them over, I'll find them myself."

He turned toward a chest of drawers, then to the closet.

"I like you, Adam," Scarlett said. "But that doesn't mean I won't hurt you. Do you honestly think I'm going to let you walk out of here with the Master Tools?"

Adam ignored Scarlett's warning and charged for the chest of drawers.

"Fool," Scarlett muttered, shaking her head. She shot Adam with a dark spell that brought him down to the floor. Cassie winced just watching it.

"Why do you insist on defying me?" Scarlett's hands hovered over Adam's body, drawing a wounded shriek from his mouth. "This pain you're feeling," she said, "I want you to understand that it's your own doing. You're making me do this to you right now."

Adam cried out like an injured animal, clawing at the floor, trying to get away.

"And if you make me destroy you," Scarlett continued, "so be it." She thrashed her fists and Adam squealed as if he'd been whipped. She did it again, and then again. Each time, Adam screamed louder, begging for Scarlett to stop.

Cassie couldn't stand by and watch him being tortured for another second. She ran at Scarlett with outstretched hands and shouted, "*Fragilis!*"

It was the same spell Scarlett had used on Cassie last time they fought. It was a black magic spell, but Cassie knew how to perform it now. She had absorbed it somehow these past few weeks.

Before Scarlett even knew what hit her, she fell to the floor beside Adam, like all the energy had drained out of her body. She struggled to lift her head, to see who'd blindsided her in her own hideout.

Cassie turned to Adam and yelled, "Get out of here!" But the moment he was up on his feet, Scarlett recited a line, "*Hoc funem est carcerem,*" and Adam flew backward onto the wooden chair across from the sofa. The threads of the chair's upholstery unraveled in thick ropes and tied Adam tightly in place.

"Really, Cassie," Scarlett said, standing. "You didn't think it would be that easy, did you?" She raised her arms and focused on Cassie, but Cassie beat her to the punch.

"*Cadunt,*" Cassie commanded. Scarlett dropped to her knees again, and then tipped over onto the ground. She fell straight-limbed and unyielding in one swift motion, the way a tree goes down in the forest.

"What were you saying about this being easy?" Cassie quipped.

Scarlett lay unmoving flat on her back.

"Untie me, Cassie!" Adam screamed. "We need to get out of here."

Cassie pretended not to hear him. At the moment she could have easily freed Adam from the ropes without even using her hands. A simple unraveling spell would have done it. But being tied up is what kept Adam safe and out of the crossfire. This fight was between her and her sister, and she was prepared to finish it right then and there.

Cassie yelled over to where Scarlett was lying on the floor. "Have you had enough yet? Or should we keep going? Because I'm just getting warmed up."

Scarlett refused to surrender. The defense spell she hollered out sounded like a cry for help, or a plea to her own body. "*Oriuntur*," Scarlett demanded, and she used every bit of strength she had to stand up again.

The book, though, Cassie noticed—*her book*—had slipped from Scarlett's grasp.

Cassie thrust her charged fingers toward its pages and called to it, "*Mihi venit!*"

To Scarlett's surprise, and much to her own, the book quivered and rose up from the floor until it was eye-level with Cassie. Then it floated across the room like a leaf caught in the wind, right into Cassie's outstretched hands.

Cassie gripped the book's soft cover and hugged it close to her chest.

Scarlett desperately cast her trembling fingers at Cassie again. "*Praestrangulo,*" she screamed. "*Caecitas!*" She was frantic, trying every spell she knew. But Cassie had the upper hand now.

"*Divorsus,*" Cassie said calmly. A simple wave of her arm blocked all of Scarlett's feeble spells.

With her father's book in hand, Cassie understood where her new power was coming from. Somehow, it had seeped into her veins those past weeks; Black John's spells were now hers. She could feel the book's power coursing through her. This was right. It was Scarlett who had to go.

"And I thought you were going to put up a fight," Cassie said, egging Scarlett on. "I mistook you for a worthy opponent."

Scarlett was running out of options. Barely able to stand, exhausted from casting too many spells, she momentarily glanced at the shallow closet closed off from the room by two folding doors.

The quick look wasn't lost on Cassie. "Hmm," she said, turning to face the closet. "I wonder what's in there. Could it be my Tools? The ones you stole from me?"

Scarlett's eyes widened, and she dashed for the closet doors.

"*Desiccare!*" Cassie shouted.

Scarlett dropped to the floor once more. Her legs and arms stiffened like the limbs of a corpse.

"I guess that answers *that*." Cassie casually walked over to Scarlett. She watched the spell collapse Scarlett's spine and wrinkle its way up the length of Scarlett's neck.

"Cassie!" Adam cried out desperately. "Untie me, now!"

Finally Scarlett's face succumbed to the spell. It dried and shriveled like a preserved peach, then turned gray and ashen—motionless as a mask, except for her eyes, which darted frantically back and forth.

"You know this already," Cassie said. "But I'll remind you again just this once. The Master Tools belong to me. And from now on, they answer only to me. And that boy over there?" She gestured to Adam. "He's mine."

Scarlett's dark eyes slowed to a stop, hardening to a stony gray that matched the rest of her desiccated body.

Cassie grinned. "Who do you think is Daddy's favorite now? I'll give you a hint: It's not you."

"Cassie," Adam called to her, but he sounded far away, as if he were at the opposite end of a long tunnel.

She knew he was there in the room with her, but at the moment he seemed small and unimportant. He may as well have not been there at all.

"You're nothing," Cassie said to Scarlett. "Nothing."

Cassie felt invincible. She could destroy Scarlett so easily now. She suddenly knew the right words. They came to her strikingly from deep within her gut. She could taste them, bitter like licorice on her tongue:

I maledicentibus vobis in mortem.

I curse you to death.

CHAPTER 18

"*Cassie!*" *Adam screamed.* "*Your eyes. You have to stop!*"

Cassie heard Adam's cries, but couldn't register their meaning. All she could see was the image of Scarlett in front of her, dead.

"You're going to kill her!" Adam screamed, just before Cassie could speak the words that would murder her sister.

Cassie sputtered, confused, as if Adam had finally shaken her awake from a nightmare.

"It's Black John. It's the darkness controlling you," Adam said. "This isn't you, Cassie."

Cassie gazed around the room like she'd never seen it before, and then at Scarlett, who was dying at her feet.

Cassie felt her own insides cave in. Her legs went soft, and she felt light-headed. Adam was right. This wasn't her.

She carefully set her father's Book of Shadows on the table and backed away from it with caution. Then she looked at Adam. "What have I done?"

Some of the color returned to Adam's face and his shoulders settled. "Not what you *almost* did, thank goodness." He took a deep breath. "I thought I'd lost you for good."

Cassie ran to Adam and wrapped her arms around him.

"There's a better way to deal with Scarlett," he said. "We'll figure out what it is together. But you have to untie me first."

Cassie's first instinct was to use magic to set Adam free, but then she thought better of it. She untied him the old-fashioned way, tugging and untwisting the ropy threads confining him to the chair until he was free.

Adam stood up and stretched his legs. He rubbed his sore, rope-burned wrists. "Where did you learn all those dark spells?" he asked. "Have you been able to translate that much of the book?"

"No. I don't know," Cassie said. "They just came to me."

"What do you mean, they just came to you? Like from inside you? Your eyes were as black as marbles."

"Adam, I don't know. Can we just focus on Scarlett right now?" Scarlett was still lying motionless on the floor, gray and desiccated.

"Will she be okay?" Adam asked.

"I think so," Cassie said. "But I can also do a reversal spell."

Adam considered their options for a minute. "Before she can move again," he said, "there's another spell I think we should try. It'll prevent her from ever returning to New Salem. What do you think? Are you up for it?"

"A magical restraining order," Cassie said. "That sounds great, but I don't think our regular magic is strong enough to work on her."

"It will be." Adam nodded toward the closet.

The Master Tools. Of course. In all the commotion, Cassie had almost forgotten about them.

Cassie stepped around Scarlett to open the closet's folding doors. She rummaged through some junk on the floor and moved around some boxes on a high shelf, and there they were. Just sitting there for the taking. The silver bracelet, the leather garter, and the sparkling diadem.

Cassie reached for each one individually. First the bracelet. She fastened it around her upper arm. Its smooth silver felt cool against her skin. Next she secured the soft leather garter on her thigh. Adam came up behind her as she reached for the diadem. He straightened it on her head for her.

"Now that's more like it," he said. "That's the Cassie I know and love."

Cassie tried to soak up the positive energy from each Tool—to feel like the Cassie Adam knew and loved. She tried her best to smile.

"I feel good," she said. "Better." Then she looked at Scarlett. "Let's try the restraining spell."

"We'll need a few things first." Adam hurried around the house, searching for supplies, digging through a few different drawers and cabinets. "I'll be right back," he said, and ran out to the front yard.

Cassie had a few moments to think about what she'd just been through. She'd come so close to killing her sister. How could Adam ever look at her the same way? How could she wear the Master Tools now, or ever be worthy of them again?

Adam returned from outside, rosy cheeked and with a fistful of dirt. "Okay," he said. "Let's give this spell a try."

He bent down to Scarlett and guided Cassie's hand to Scarlett's forehead. "You hold her here and concentrate.

It's important that your intentions remain clear, Cassie, can you do that?"

"Yes," Cassie said easily. But she knew she would really have to try.

Scarlett's forehead was cold and hard; it was almost like touching a corpse. Adam lit a candle and swung it above Scarlett's body, back and forth from the top of her head, down to the bottoms of her feet. Then he recited the chant. "I banish you from New Salem, Scarlett, with the power of fire."

Cassie imagined a soothing white light. She pictured it growing brighter and more intense until it had enveloped not only Scarlett but herself and Adam as well.

Adam secured the lit candle in a holder upon the floor, just north of Scarlett's head. Then he scattered the fistful of dirt he'd collected from the front yard onto the floor, encircling Scarlett within it. He said, "I banish you from New Salem, Scarlett, with the power of earth."

Cassie could smell the loamy trail of dirt and was reminded of the elemental wholesomeness of the earth, the cleanliness of stark terrain. She imagined the white light filling the whole room, and then the entire house from the inside out.

Next Adam reached for a cup of water he'd set on the

table. He dipped his hand deep into the cup and then sprinkled drops of water, like rain, over Scarlett's skin. "I banish you from New Salem, Scarlett, with the power of water," he said.

Finally Adam went to open the front door of the house and a large window on the opposite side, creating a strong cross-breeze in the main room. The rush of air blew out the candle he'd set on the floor. "I banish you from New Salem, Scarlett, with the power of air," he said.

He placed his hands gently over Cassie's, joining her in holding Scarlett's forehead. He closed his eyes and said, "Fire, earth, water, and air, and the power of the Master Tools, mote it be."

Scarlett stirred and Adam opened his eyes. "That's it," he said.

Cassie let her hands drop to her sides. "Did it work?"

"We'll find out," Adam said. "But after all this, I don't think she'll be much of a threat anymore."

Cassie nodded, but she wasn't so sure. She couldn't imagine a time when Scarlett would no longer be a menace.

Adam picked up Black John's Book of Shadows and gestured to the door. "What do you say we get out of here?"

Cassie looked Scarlett over one last time and nodded.

She went to the front door and put one hand on the knob. With her other hand, she waved her fingers at Scarlett. *"I tollere malum incantatores,"* she said, the words of the reversal spell.

Scarlett's color came back and she gasped for breath just as Cassie and Adam stepped outside, slamming the door behind them.

CHAPTER 19

Once they were back at Cassie's house, Adam and Cassie took a few minutes to sit down on the front porch swing and collect themselves. It was dark, and they both began to yawn now that their adrenaline had settled. Adam turned to Cassie and shyly smiled. "Thanks for saving my butt back there."

Cassie was comforted by Adam's ability to make light of the situation—it meant he was beginning to get over the shock of seeing her overcome by dark magic. Maybe things could finally go back to normal for them. But first she had to address what he'd done.

"I owed you one," Cassie said. "But it was stupid of

you to go after Scarlett by yourself. You could have been killed."

"It didn't seem stupid in my head. I knew where you'd hidden the book, and I had hoped to trade it for the Master Tools."

"But do you know how dangerous that book could be in Scarlett's possession?"

"To be honest with you, Cassie, I did it because I wanted to get the book away from you. I thought getting it out of your hands might save you from its darkness. You have to believe me. I was trying to help."

Cassie recalled how the book seemed to be summoning her each time Scarlett turned one of its pages, how it beckoned her to attack Scarlett with black magic.

"After how I acted back there," Cassie said, "I'm worried it's too late. I think the book has done its damage."

"No. Don't talk like that," Adam said. "It was a close call, but nothing irreparable was done."

Cassie's heart instantly flooded with regret. She knew this was the moment to tell Adam what had happened the night before with Nick. If she didn't tell him now, she may never have the courage again.

"I did do something irreparable," she said. "I wish it wasn't true, but it is."

"What did you do?" Adam asked, but when Cassie remained silent, he tried a less accusatory tone. "Whatever it is, we can work through it," he said. "As long as you're honest with me." Cassie still picked up on the hint of dread in his voice.

"Last night," Cassie said, feeling sick with shame, "I kissed Nick."

Adam's whole body constricted. "I can't believe him," he mumbled to the air.

"It was all me," Cassie insisted. "Nick was a perfect gentleman. I practically forced myself on him."

Adam glared straight ahead for a few seconds.

"I am so unbelievably sorry," Cassie said.

She was hoping Adam would say something in return, but he was dead silent.

"I know it's no excuse," Cassie continued. "But when it happened it was like the book was making me want to hurt you. Like it had taken over my mind and my body. I couldn't control myself."

"I get it," Adam said. His voice cracked with emotion. "I don't want to hear any more."

"But I want you to understand that I didn't mean for it to happen. That's not how I feel about Nick. I know that still doesn't make it okay, and you have every right to hate me—"

"I can never hate you," Adam said. "But I can't say I'm not a little hurt."

Cassie placed her hand on Adam's knee, relieved he was at least speaking to her. "It will never happen again," she said. "I promise."

"I know it won't happen again. Especially after we figure out what to do with that book." Adam glanced at the book, which was resting between them alongside the Master Tools. "It's the book I hate, not you."

A pang of worry shot through Cassie's chest. What if Adam's resentment for the book caused him to do something drastic? He wouldn't try to destroy it, would he?

"We've both made mistakes recently," Adam said. "And we have bigger concerns to deal with. One kiss is hardly the worst of them."

"Bigger concerns," Cassie said. "Like me being altogether evil."

Adam shook his head. "You're not evil, Cassie. One day, I promise, our lives will be normal enough that I will sufficiently freak out if you kiss another guy of your own volition, not because a cursed book made you do it."

Cassie had to laugh as Adam gave the porch swing a little nudge, sending them gently back and then forward again.

Adam took a long breath in, held it, and exhaled heavily, as if he were blowing out every hurt feeling and negative thought within him. He looked longingly at Cassie and then leaned over and kissed her.

Cassie had never felt so gratified by a kiss in all her life. For a few blissful minutes she forgot all her troubles. She was healed. She was with Adam and that was all that mattered.

Adam must have felt it, too, because his passion for Cassie now was pressing and pleading. He kissed her like he hadn't seen her in years, like he wanted to erase her kiss with Nick from her mind and claim her for himself.

But Cassie finally, reluctantly pulled away. "We should go inside," she said. "We can continue this later in private, after we tell everyone about getting the Master Tools back."

Adam agreed and the two of them got up from the swing. They straightened their clothes and gathered the book and Tools to carry them inside.

"They're going to freak out when they see these," Adam said, holding the Tools up like a trophy. They glistened in the moonlight.

"I know," Cassie said. "But maybe we can leave out the worst parts of the story about how we got them back?"

Adam didn't argue. The two of them made their way through the house and jogged down the basement stairs. They excitedly revealed the hidden door—but on the opposite side, they found an empty room.

"Hello!" Cassie called out. "Come out, come out, wherever you are."

Within a few seconds her joviality was quelled. This was no game of hide-and-seek. Not a single member of the Circle was to be found in the room.

There were laptops left open and dishes with food on them still on the table. Laurel's desk lamp hadn't been turned off and neither had the light in the bathroom.

Cassie set down her father's book and the Master Tools, and a knot formed in her throat. "Where could they have gone?" she said. But she couldn't state the worry nagging her: If their friends were discovered, they most likely had been killed.

"There's no way the hunters got in here." Adam scrutinized the room in a desperate search for clues. "They must be with the rest of the Circle. Text Diana."

Cassie rummaged through her bag for her phone. She'd silenced it on her way to Stockbridge and forgot to turn the ringer back on. Now a list of urgent text messages, mostly from Nick, stared her in the face.

She scanned through them nervously. "Faye went after the principal," she said to Adam. "The rest of them are chasing after her, to keep her from doing anything stupid."

"Too late." Adam slammed his hand down on the table. "That half-translated witch-hunter curse will never work."

"The last text says they were headed to the school." Cassie stuffed her phone back into her pocket. "It was sent twenty minutes ago."

Without another word the two of them rushed upstairs. Cassie felt heat stealing into her face and a twisting panic in her stomach. She tried to catch her breath once they were inside Adam's car, but it was no use.

Adam floored the accelerator pedal, his eyes wild. Cassie watched the speedometer arc steadily from left to right. He had to be driving ninety miles per hour, but it still didn't feel fast enough. If they didn't make it to the school in time . . . Cassie couldn't fathom it.

But she had to be mentally prepared. Even if their friends were lying dead on the ground when they arrived, Cassie still had to be ready to fight.

CHAPTER 20

Arriving at the school, Adam and Cassie were unsure where to look first. The sky was dark as midnight, but there was enough security lighting to give them a decent view of the grounds. From the parking lot they scanned the empty bleachers and vacant football field. They checked the perimeter of the building, and the outer wing where the principal's office was located.

"Do you think they're inside?" Cassie asked. "Maybe we should split up."

"Up there," Adam said. "I think that's them."

There was movement on the roof of the building, barely visible shadows, but clashing voices echoed down to the ground. Cassie pushed away her fear and forced the trembling within her stomach to steady her. If there were sounds of a scuffle, that meant there was still a fight.

Adam rushed for the rusty fire escape that ran up the side of the building and Cassie followed just behind him. They quieted their steps as they neared the top. There, they discovered Diana, Melanie, Chris, Doug, and Sean hiding behind the metal railing.

Diana noticed them and put her finger over her lips to indicate they should be quiet. Cassie and Adam moved to where they could view the action at the center of the roof. It was a formidable sight.

Nick, Faye, Laurel, Deborah, and Suzan were aligned in a tight defensive circle. They appeared trapped and powerless, as if they'd been confined to a cage. And their marks glowed bright on their chests, like iridescent hearts beating over their clothes.

The hunter marks must shine in the presence of the relics, Cassie thought. Three hunters surrounded the group, and each of them held a gray stone carved into the dreadful shape of the hunter symbol.

It was the principal and two others—one man and one woman. Cassie wondered where Max was. Did Diana have something to do with his absence? But there wasn't any time for questions.

The man was older—Cassie would even call him elderly. He had long white hair and eyes the color of ice. The woman appeared to be around Cassie's mother's age. She was rail thin and had mousy brown hair and brown eyes, but there was no mistaking the resemblance between the two.

Through her research, Laurel had identified two of the last remaining hunters as Jedediah Felton—an ancestor of one of the most feared hunter families in history—and his daughter, Louvera Felton. Now here they were in the flesh.

The Feltons didn't look as Cassie had expected they would. They seemed so normal. In Cassie's imagination, the hunters were giant tribal-looking men wearing some sort of traditional garb, like a robe a martial-arts master would wear. But these hunters would have passed for three average adults if not for the ancient relics they wielded like weapons.

"They don't look so tough," Adam said. "Without those stones, they'd have nothing on us."

"But those stones contain power that goes back over six hundred years," Diana whispered. "Isn't that what Laurel said?"

Cassie nodded.

"What are they mumbling?" Adam asked. "Do you think it's the killing spell?"

The hunters chanted in a low hum, repeating an ominous phrase:

> *I sum eius agens,*
> *I occidere in eius nomen——*
> *I sum eius agens,*
> *I occidere in eius nomen——*

Just then, all five of their friends on the center of the roof dropped to their knees. They held their skulls as if they were suffering from terrible migraines.

"It has to be the killing curse," Cassie said. She made a motion to lunge forward and reveal herself, but Diana grabbed her by the arm and pulled her back.

"Wait," she said. "If we show ourselves, we'll be trapped just like the others. The witch-hunter curse we translated must not have worked. Otherwise Faye and the rest of them wouldn't be in this state."

Laurel and Suzan were writhing on the ground at the hunters' feet. Faye was on her knees, screaming out in pain. Nick cringed, holding his head like it was bleeding, and Deborah looked like she had passed out from the torture.

"We have to try something," Cassie said. "We probably only have a few minutes, maybe even seconds."

"A blocking spell," Adam said. "To turn the energy of their curse back on them. With the seven of us, we might have enough power." He closed his eyes and reached for Cassie's hands. "Repeat after me: *Hunters, disperse. We reverse your curse.*"

The group of them linked arms and did as Adam said, though Cassie didn't have much faith that such a generic spell could be strong enough to have an effect on those ancient relics. Still, she concentrated all her energy on the chant. "*Hunters, disperse. We reverse your curse.*"

At first nothing happened, but then the hunters paused. Continuing their low hum, they looked from side to side. The magic had caught their attention, but they continued with the chant.

Then Cassie felt a change. A heated power. Not knowing where it came from, a string of new words sprouted from her mouth. "*Venatores dispergam. Nos vertite maledictionem.*" The words were rasping, guttural sounds that rose from deep in her throat. She immediately recognized the feeling as dark magic, but she allowed it to come. Her whole being trembled with a painful ecstasy.

The hunters were truly startled now. They halted their chanting and searched the shadows for the source of the spell. They waved their relics, but they seemed not to understand what they were feeling. They only knew it wasn't good.

"*Venatores dispergam. Nos vertite maledictionem,*" Cassie said again.

Mr. Boylan scolded the others for breaking their concentration. "Focus!" he shouted. "We're not finished yet."

But within seconds the old man stopped reciting the curse. His face reddened and he clutched his chest. "It's an ancient," he said. "I don't know how, but I'm sure of it."

Jedediah doubled over, and began pounding on his own heart. "Find him," he screamed out to the others.

But Cassie continued uttering her dark words, louder now that she saw how well they were working. Adam and the others stood silently by, their arms still linked.

Louvera made a motion to go to her father's aid, but then she also grabbed her chest as if she were having a heart attack. She gasped for air, unable to speak.

Mr. Boylan was visibly weakening. His spine curved downward, bending his usually rigid posture into a rounded question mark. All the color had drained from his face and his whole body shook with exhaustion.

Jedediah climbed to his hands and knees and began crawling to the hatch door in the roof that led down into the school building.

Louvera cried out with whatever air she had left, "Release them!" She choked and crawled in the same direction as the old man, and slid down the gaping hole in the roof to safety.

But the principal refused to run away. He continued reciting the curse, holding tight to his relic, as he fell to his knees.

Cassie took a few steps forward, directing her words straight for him. He tried to stand back up, but fell down again.

One by one, the Circle members who had fallen began slowly rising to their feet. Faye and Laurel, then Nick and Suzan, and finally Deborah were shaking off the pain that had debilitated them only minutes earlier.

Cassie could feel herself growing stronger as Mr. Boylan became weaker, as if she were sucking out his power and keeping it for her own use. She watched him shrivel before her eyes, panting like a cowardly animal. He clutched his chest and cried out. But Cassie felt no remorse for him whatsoever. She was only disgusted by his frailty. She was sure he would remain there withering to his death, and she would let him.

Then, one last time, he got to his feet. He wobbled and, still unsure where the real opposition was coming from, he honed in on Faye. In a final desperate effort, he cast all his remaining energy at her, shouting the killing curse one last time as loud as he could.

Before Faye knew what was coming, Suzan leapt in front of her, knocking her out of the way and onto the ground.

His power spent, Boylan finally retreated. Defenseless and shambling, he dragged himself away, across the rooftop, and down the same escape route as his fellow hunters.

Cassie continued moving toward him, still uttering the curse.

"Cassie," Adam called out. "That's enough. He's gone."

But Cassie couldn't stop—the words continued coursing through her like a piano that played itself. She didn't want the sensation to end.

Adam grabbed her by the shoulders and shook her furiously. "Snap out of it," he shouted. "The hunters are gone."

Somehow Adam's words reached Cassie through the

long tunnel she'd gotten lost in. She snapped to consciousness and looked around hazily.

Chris and Doug came into view, then Sean and Melanie, and even through her clouded vision Cassie could see the hunter symbols glowing on their clothes. Each of them had been marked. Then Cassie turned to Diana and saw that she, too, had the symbol glowing on her sleeve. And so did Adam. Cassie pointed to it, shaking.

"I know," Adam said. "I saw it."

Then Cassie looked down and saw the front of her shirt gleaming as well. Now they were all on equal footing. The entire Circle had been marked. A strange calm came over Cassie, like the worst had finally happened and now they could move forward—but then Faye shrieked in a haunted pitch that made Cassie's blood run cold.

Faye was kneeling, shaking, over an unmoving Suzan.

Everything started to blur as they all rushed to where Suzan was lying. Adam reached her first. He dropped to his knees and checked her neck and wrist for a pulse. Then he listened to see if she was breathing.

"Call an ambulance!" he screamed, but nobody moved. Suzan's eyes had already glassed over. Her face had hardened to a lifeless mask.

"She's dead," Faye said, to herself as much as to Adam. "She died saving my life."

"No." Adam shuddered, refusing to accept the truth. He tried CPR. He tried mouth-to-mouth resuscitation. Finally he just pounded on Suzan's chest. But it was too late.

Cassie kneeled down to see for herself what none of them could bear to register. The witch hunter's death symbol was glowing bright on Suzan's forehead.

CHAPTER 21

A warm breeze rustled the graveyard's foliage as the Circle and Suzan's father gathered for her burial. It was an impossibly sunny day, which only made Cassie feel guilty that she could enjoy it when Suzan couldn't. Suzan had been such a lighthearted person, always able to find the fun in any situation. How was it possible that they could all be standing here now beneath the bright sun, while Suzan would be buried beneath heavy black dirt? It wasn't fair, and nothing anyone said would make sense of it.

The graveyard was mostly flat, comprised of a few small ponds and crooked streams. The jagged coastline was visible in the distance to the east. To the west were wooded,

---

rolling hills. And prevailing over all of it were the granite cliffs in the far north. This was a beautiful place. Why were such wonders made so much more visible by death and loss? Was that why tragedies happened? To open our eyes to the miraculous, to force us to appreciate joy?

Only Deborah had the courage to say a brief eulogy over Suzan's casket, to reach for a few words that might capture what the whole Circle was feeling. She cleared her throat and looked affectionately at Suzan's father.

"Suzan was easy to underestimate," she said, and a few people giggled. "In fact, Suzan wanted you to underestimate her, so she could later surprise you with her wit and intelligence, her goodness, her generosity, and let's not forget, her sarcasm. Beneath all her fancy clothes and makeup, Suzan was a pure soul." Deborah was choking back tears now. "She was pure through and through. And we're all going to miss her very much."

They all began to cry, but Faye was the most distraught of all. She could barely keep herself upright, she was so overcome with grief. To keep her sobbing from disrupting the ceremony, she staggered off to the side to lean against a barren tree.

Cassie went to her. She approached her the way she would have approached an injured street cat, with

carefulness and caution, fully prepared to back off if necessary. She tried putting her arm around her, but Faye
immediately pushed her away. "I don't want your pity. Just
leave me alone."

"Faye," Cassie said. "None of this is your fault. You
can't be blaming yourself."

Faye stared viciously at the ground. "It should have
been me. I wish it was me in that box right now."

"Faye."

"No, Cassie. It's easy for you to say it's nobody's fault.
You saved the day. You're the hero. But I'm the reason
Suzan was on that roof to begin with. And then she
threw herself in front of the killing curse to save me. So
don't stand there and try to make me feel better. I don't
deserve it."

Cassie could understand the sentiment. She didn't
want to feel better either. And if Faye wished to punish
herself, there was nothing Cassie could do to convince
her otherwise. She took a step closer to Faye but didn't
attempt to touch her this time. She just stood near her
quietly and respectfully, hoping at the very least to make
Faye feel less alone in her remorse.

They watched the remainder of the service together
from afar. After the casket was lowered into the ground,

there was nothing left for anyone to do but file back to their cars.

Cassie took Faye's hand and guided her across the grass to the rest of the group. With her other hand, she reached for Adam. Together, the eleven of them walked solemnly across the graveyard, but Cassie felt as if each step took them further away from one another. This devastation had broken their bond and weakened their allegiance.

Then Cassie looked down at her and Adam's intertwined fingers. She willed it to be there. The silver cord. But nothing appeared.

The town of New Salem oddly came to life around funerals. People Cassie had never even seen before poured into Suzan's house with flowers and food for Suzan's dad. He was polite, but dazed. It might take weeks for the reality of Suzan's death to actually hit him. Cassie wished she could go to him now and offer him some kind of explanation for what had happened to his little girl. He must have so many questions. But Cassie restrained herself. It was probably better to leave those things unsaid. None of it really added up to an explanation anyhow.

Diana huddled close to Cassie and whispered in her

ear. "See those?" she said, pointing to a bouquet of lilies. "They're from Max."

Cassie could see Diana was hurting. Not having Max nearby when she needed him the most couldn't have been easy. This day would have been impossible for Cassie to endure without Adam. But then again, Adam wasn't the Circle's sworn enemy.

Diana touched one of the lilies longingly. "I broke it off with him, you know."

Cassie tried not to appear relieved.

"After what happened with Suzan, I realized how dangerous it really was," Diana continued. "I told him I needed to stand with my Circle."

"And he's okay with that?"

"He doesn't have a choice," Diana said, but she gazed around the room as if she were still hoping Max might step inside at any moment.

Cassie could relate. She had given up Adam once for the good of the Circle and her friendship with Diana. She searched her mind for the right thing to say. Max hadn't been on the roof the night of their battle, so maybe he wasn't so bad after all—maybe he was having second thoughts about being a hunter. But Cassie still couldn't ignore the facts: It was Max who'd marked Faye. It was

Max's father who'd killed Suzan—Suzan, who they'd just buried less than an hour before. Cassie couldn't help but be glad Diana had broken up with him, at least for the time being.

"Look, Diana," Cassie said. "None of us knows what the future holds. What's going to happen between you and Max down the road isn't something we can predict. But today, you have your friends. And we're here for you—we have to be, now more than ever."

"You're right. And I'm grateful. Believe me, I am." Diana paused. "It's just that sometimes I wish everything could just be normal. Do you know what I mean?"

"Well," Cassie said, looking over at Adam. He was greeting strangers at the door, thanking them for their casseroles and flowers, directing them toward the sitting room. He was always the helper, always the gentle knight. How could Cassie judge Diana harshly for choosing a complicated person to love, when she knew it was hardly a choice at all?

"You know what I think?" Cassie put her arm around Diana and brought her in for a hug. "I think sometimes, normal is overrated."

CHAPTER 22

Later that night, after the mourners had gone home, the Circle convened in Diana's living room. They sat motionless, leaning on one another, staring into space as if waiting for something none of them could name. They listened to the sound of the driving rain on the roof and the savage gusts of wind buffeting the bay window. Outside, the night sky had turned pink in the storm: Suzan's favorite color.

Nobody knew what to say, and there was much not being said. Those unspoken words hung in the air like ghosts in their midst: that it could have been any one of them who'd been killed. That if Cassie hadn't shown up, they'd all have witch-hunter death symbols glowing on their foreheads. It was a strange mind-set, to be both grieving for the death of their friend while also giving thanks that they'd been spared.

Faye sat hugging her knees to her chest on the end of the couch, separate from the others. Her eyes were blank and drooping with exhaustion. Cassie understood it would be a long time before Faye was acting like herself again, and even then, she might never be the same.

Diana took a deep breath and looked at the group. "One of our own is dead," she said. "The Circle has been broken." Her Book of Shadows was at her side. She picked it up and brought it into her lap. "I don't want to talk about this any more than you do, but we have to find out what happens now that our Circle is incomplete."

"It means we're weak again," Deborah said. "Like we were before we initiated Cassie, before we were whole."

Melanie nodded. "This is the worst time for us to have an unbound Circle, with the combined threat of the hunters and Scarlett. I don't mean to sound cold, but we need to initiate someone in Suzan's place as soon as possible."

Laurel's eyes welled up with tears. Cassie couldn't

blame her. She could hardly stand to think about these technicalities either. She wanted to go home, take a hot bath, and bury her head in her mother's shoulder. But she had to stand by her friends—she had to try to help in whatever way she could.

Cassie offered the Circle the only information she knew. "Scarlett said whoever dies in a bound Circle has to be replaced by someone of their own bloodline. Whoever's next in their family lineage. So we're not going to have much say in the matter of who fills Suzan's place."

"Right," Adam said, responding to Cassie. "But Suzan had no siblings or other family that we know about. So what happens now?"

"Maybe it becomes a wild card," Nick suggested. "And we get to choose whoever we want."

"I wish that were the case, but I'd be shocked if it were that simple." Diana flipped through her Book of Shadows, searching for something. Within a few seconds she found the page she was looking for.

"This is a family tree spell," she said, holding the book up for all to see and then setting it back down on her lap. "It could help us fill in any blanks in Suzan's ancestry."

Adam read the spell over Diana's shoulder. "It can definitely tell us who would be next in line. If there is anyone."

"I'm pretty sure Suzan's bloodline ended with her," Deborah said. "She was the only child of two only children, wasn't she?"

"We can't be too sure." Adam looked up from the book. "Suzan's family was notoriously tight-lipped. Her father refused to talk about the past with her at all. I think checking her family tree is worth a try."

Diana read over the detailed instructions. "It seems simple enough. All we need is some canvas paper and . . ." Her voice trailed off.

"What?" Sean asked, sounding like he sensed the worst.

"We need something of Suzan's," Diana said quietly. "Something containing DNA. Like her blood."

The room fell silent. Awful visions of Suzan's body buried tightly beneath the cold ground rushed through Cassie's mind. "There's no way," she said. "Forget it."

But Laurel quickly got up and ran into the other room. She returned carrying Suzan's soft leather purse. "I brought this so we could perform a deep peace ritual tonight. As a memorial with some of her favorite things."

Laurel opened the purse so they could all view its

contents. It was a mishmash of makeup, bubble gum, and crumpled up Twinkie wrappers. Cassie felt a lump form in her throat. There was something sacrilegious about going through a deceased person's personal items. The purse even smelled like Suzan.

"I don't think you're going to find any blood in there," Cassie said. "At least I hope you don't."

"That's not what I'm looking for." Laurel lifted Suzan's hairbrush out from the bottom of the purse. She pulled a few tangled strands of Suzan's strawberry-blond hair out of its bristles. "There's your DNA," she said to Diana. "It'll work the same as a blood sample."

"Laurel, you're a genius." Diana bolted to her desk drawer to retrieve a canvas art pad. She flipped through the pad, past a number of charcoal drawings and acrylic paintings, until she found a blank page. She tore it out carefully and brought it back to the group. Then she continued reading from her Book of Shadows.

"We'll still need ink," Diana said. "But it has to come from something Suzan had direct contact with. Is there a pen inside her purse? If she used it recently it might still contain some of her energy."

Laurel dug through the bag, but she couldn't find a pen. "No luck," she said. "But this might work." She offered Diana a bottle of Suzan's nail polish. It was the same color she'd painted her nails earlier that week—sparkle-flecked magenta.

Diana took the bottle from Laurel and uncapped it. "She definitely had contact with this."

Cassie and the others gathered around Diana, forming a circle, as she prepared the spell. She placed the canvas flat on the floor and scattered Suzan's hair on it, as her Book of Shadows instructed. Then she trickled a few drops of the nail polish on the center of the page and said:

Reveal to us Suzan's family tree.
And who our new Circle member will be.

Immediately, pinkish purple lines soaked into the veins of the paper like blood. Up from the bottom of the page, a tree began to draw itself in watery magenta strokes. It was thick at its base and grew upward and out in long stalks, spreading across the entire canvas. Branches formed and then names attached to each branch.

"It's working," Diana said. "I don't believe it."

Cassie watched each generation of Suzan's family

grow from the tree like blossoming fruit. The first names
to appear dated back three hundred years, which
meant Suzan's ancestors must have been among New
Salem's founding families. The tree grew fast through
the decades and seemed to be picking up speed as it
neared the present. By the time Suzan's parents' names
appeared, almost every inch of paper had been inked
over in fine print.

"Linda Forsythe," Laurel said. "That was Suzan's
mother who passed away in the storm. We would have
known her as Linda Whittier."

"Forsythe?" Cassie said aloud, but nobody heard her.
She hadn't remembered until now that the surname
Whittier came from Suzan's father's side. She hadn't
given any thought at all to Suzan's mother's bloodline.

"Forsythe?" Cassie said again. Her stomach twisted at
the sight of it. "That was Suzan's mother's maiden name?"

But no one responded. Everyone was too focused on
the next line being drawn to the tree.

Linda Forsythe's name connected to her husband's
and then branched out to form Suzan's name. But then
another branch formed from Linda Forsythe's name:
Laura Forsythe.

"Who's that?" Melanie asked.

"It looks like Suzan's mother had a sibling we didn't know about. A sister. Forsythe . . ." Diana said, turning to Cassie, her face pale. "Hold on. Isn't that—"

The final name on the tree brought Diana to a deathly silence. It branched downward from Laura Forsythe's name and glowed in bright magenta: *Scarlett Forsythe*.

"No," Cassie said. But she watched in horror as one final deep red line connected Suzan's name to Scarlett's. "This can't be right," she said. "Suzan and Scarlett can't be related."

"Suzan and Scarlett were cousins?" Adam said.

"Does this mean what I think it means?" Laurel asked.

Cassie broke into a cold sweat. So that was the name of Scarlett's mother. Laura Forsythe. The woman who'd sparred with Cassie's own mother over Black John's affections. She had run away from New Salem, Cassie knew that. Her mother said she'd disappeared, never to be heard from again. But here she was now, long after she'd died, appearing once more as a crucial element to both the past and the future.

"Suzan definitely had no idea she had an aunt," Melanie said. "And Scarlett must not have known either. Or else she would have gone after Suzan the same way she went after Cassie for her spot in the Circle."

Diana picked up the canvas and stared at Scarlett's name. "And now she's gotten it anyway. She's our new member, whether we like it or not."

"Unless we don't initiate her," Cassie said.

CHAPTER 23

"If we don't initiate Scarlett into the Circle," Adam said, "we'll be much weaker when we're fighting the hunters."

The rain continued pouring down in sheets. Cassie watched it through the large bay window in Diana's living room. It was better than staring down at the magenta ink of Scarlett's name on Suzan's family tree.

"We have to initiate her," Melanie said. "Nothing matters more than defeating the hunters, especially after what they did to Suzan."

"But we know she has ulterior motives and can't be trusted," Nick said. "Remember, she wanted Cassie's place in the Circle so she could use our Circle's power for her own agenda. She'd be as bad as initiating Black John himself."

Melanie scoffed at Nick. "That's an overstatement if I've ever heard one."

Cassie wanted this conversation to stop. The sky outside had settled to a deep purple and the clouds rolled and shifted in ever-changing shapes. Cassie saw a heart and then a castle, and then nothing, just a sheet of gray. Her mind wandered and an image flashed into view: herself back at the Mission House on the brink of killing Scarlett. But this time she'd gone through with it. She completed the killing spell and Scarlett's eyes had glassed over the way Suzan's had up on the roof, and then she stiffened to a lifeless statue. Cassie imagined exactly what it would feel like for Scarlett to be gone forever—how the Circle would be free at last.

That's it, Cassie thought. That was the solution. She would have to kill Scarlett. Then they could take their chances with another lost family member to be next in line for the Circle.

But then she shook the idea from her mind. *No,* she told herself. *Send light to that dark thought, and cast it away.*

Cassie knew she had to fight off every evil intention the moment it appeared now, before it could really get to her and take hold.

"Cassie," Adam said. "Are you okay? You're as pale as a ghost."

"I'm fine." But the faintness of Cassie's voice gave her away.

"See," Melanie said. "Even Cassie is weaker now. I told you."

"I'm not weaker," Cassie shot back.

But Melanie was adamant. "Yes, you are. We all are."

"Let's just see about that." Chris directed his attention to the bowl of fruit on Diana's coffee table. "Who wants to see me levitate an apple?" he asked. But seconds passed and nothing happened. The apple didn't move, and Chris grew more and more frustrated as the clock continued to tick.

Melanie crossed her arms over her chest, looking smug.

"Maybe if we both try," Doug said, going to his brother's side. He focused his attention on the fruit as well. With their combined powers, the apple began to shiver. It lifted from the bowl for a brief second, but then it dropped back down.

"Shoot." Chris was breathless with fatigue. "We almost had it."

"Thank you for proving just how powerless we are," Nick said. He looked worriedly at Cassie. "We may actually be weaker than we were before you came to town."

Cassie returned her gaze to the window and took a deep breath. It was becoming more and more clear that their only option wasn't destroying Scarlett. It was going against all logic and asking her to join them.

"We can barely do the simplest everyday magic with an incomplete Circle," Melanie said. "Let alone anything strong enough to fight off the hunters. I say we initiate Scarlett, defeat the hunters, and then figure out what to do with her later."

"What do you mean, 'figure out what to do with her later'?" Diana narrowed her eyes at Melanie. "Once she's initiated, we're bound to her. You know that. Using her and then betraying her would compromise the integrity of our Circle. Not to mention our self-respect."

That's probably what Scarlett will do to us, Cassie thought, but saying so would only make things worse. She stood up and took the center of the room.

"There is no good decision to make here," she said.

"Only a less bad one. As much as I hate to admit this, I think we do need Scarlett."

Nick's jaw tightened as he ground his teeth. "I don't want her as a member," he said. "There must be another option."

"It's Scarlett or no one," Adam said, refusing to make eye contact with Nick as he addressed the group. "We don't have to trust her, but I think we do have to initiate her. You know what they say about keeping your enemies close. Well, we can't keep her much closer than in our Circle. At least she'll be somewhere we can keep an eye on her."

"Great," Nick said. "So we can have a front-row seat as she takes control of us."

"Now hold on." Diana raised her arms to quiet both of them. "There are eleven of us and one Scarlett. What makes you so sure it'll be that easy for her to take control of us?"

"Yeah," Sean said. "One bad seed can't spoil the bunch, otherwise Faye would have ruined our Circle long ago."

Faye glared at Sean as Diana continued.

"My point is, we know what Scarlett is capable of, so we're less likely to fall for any of her tricks. And don't forget, we have the Master Tools back in our possession."

Nick considered Diana's argument for a few seconds before conceding. "Fine," he said. "If Cassie's willing to take a chance on Scarlett, then I'm with her."

"Do we all agree, then?" Adam asked.

Nobody spoke out to disagree, which was as close to consensus as they were going to get.

"Good. It's settled," Adam said. "Cassie and I will take care of telling Scarlett the news and bringing her back to New Salem tomorrow."

As the group started to split up and head home for the night, the full impact of the decision sunk in. Had she really agreed to bring the other girl Adam's soul was connected to back into her life? The girl who had tried to kill her, and whom she had tried to kill? It was like restriking a dulled match just to see what would burn.

Cassie reached for Adam's hand and squeezed it. "I'll catch up with you a little later," she said. "I want to have a word with Diana."

Adam kissed her on the lips without question, so she didn't have to explain exactly *why* she wanted to speak to Diana. She didn't have to justify her father's Book of Shadows shoved deep into the bottom of her tote bag. She simply waited for everyone to trickle out of Diana's house until it was just the two of them.

"I thought you left with Adam," Diana said, when she realized Cassie had been lingering.

"Can we talk?" Cassie asked.

Diana nervously glanced around the living room even though they were alone, perhaps because she thought Cassie was going to ask her about Max. "Let's go up to my bedroom," she said, leading Cassie to the stairs.

It had been a long time since Cassie and Diana hung out on Diana's bed sharing secrets. After only a few moments of sitting there, Cassie was overwhelmed with longing for those simpler times. Before Scarlett had entered their lives, and even further back, before Adam had become an issue between them.

Diana huddled close to Cassie and asked, "Do you think Suzan's father knew about Laura Forsythe? Or that she'd had a daughter?"

"My guess is he never knew Scarlett existed," Cassie said. "But even if he did, it's ancient history now."

Diana nodded. "It's just so strange, how connected we all are, even when we don't know it. And even when we don't want to be."

Cassie sensed Diana was referring to more than just

their familial lines. "I get the feeling you're thinking about Max," she said. "And the silver cord."

Diana got quiet and Cassie had the urge to tell her all about the cord between Adam and Scarlett. She wanted to cry about it on Diana's shoulder until she delivered some typical words of Diana wisdom that would make it all better. Unfortunately, there were more pressing issues to deal with.

Cassie dug through her bag until she retrieved her father's book. She held it out to Diana. "Will you hold on to this for me? To keep it away from me for a little while?"

Diana eyed the book carefully, and then gently accepted it from Cassie's hands. "Of course. But why?"

Lines of worry creased Diana's forehead as Cassie described how she had felt on the roof when she used dark magic against the hunters. Cassie also told her what had happened with Scarlett in Stockbridge.

"I went into a trance," Cassie said. "And I almost killed Scarlett. I know it's because of the book. It's doing things to my mind."

Diana nodded gravely. "Like Adam said, you're bound to the book now. And we still don't fully understand what that means."

"But the worst part," Cassie said, "is that it feels really good when I'm like that. It's the most seductive pleasure—I can't even describe it. And it's only afterward, after I snap out of it, that I feel bad." Cassie looked down, ashamed.

"Hey." Diana put her arm around her. "We've all succumbed to temptation at one time or another. Even when we know it can be damaging."

"But I'm afraid one of these days I'll take it too far. What if I do something I can't take back—or worse, what if I can't get myself back? Every time it happens I feel like I'm going in deeper and deeper."

"You don't have to worry," Diana said. "I'll keep the book safe, and together we'll keep you safe."

Cassie felt better already. If there was anyone on earth who could be trusted with the book, it was Diana. But she still felt the need to give Diana a stern warning. "You have to let me know if anything out of the ordinary happens, do you understand? If you start feeling strange, or if it seems to be speaking to you."

Diana nodded solemnly.

"If that happens, we'll find something else to do with it," Cassie said. "I don't want you going through what I have."

"Neither do I," Diana said, trying to make light of the heavy situation. "Trust me. I've had my fair share of transgressions lately as it is."

"And whatever you do," Cassie said, "don't let Faye know you have it. In fact, don't let anybody know. Not even Adam."

Diana hesitated but then agreed. "It'll be our secret."

CHAPTER 24

Adam and Cassie drove in nervous silence over the bridge toward the Mission House.

Small talk felt too trivial, and there was nothing left to be said about the benefits and disadvantages of bringing Scarlett back to New Salem. Better to mutely admire the scenery.

Cassie observed the sugar maples glowing red beneath the sun on both sides of the highway. They were tall, graceful trees, dignified almost—a vast change in landscape from the wharves and rocky beaches on the island. The Mission House wasn't far now. As they drew closer, Cassie clung to an unvoiced hope—that Scarlett wouldn't be at the house when they arrived. The Circle couldn't initiate her until they found her. Prolonging the inevitable wasn't a solution, Cassie knew, but a little more time might help her get used to the whole idea. Just because Cassie had convinced the Circle to take a chance on Scarlett didn't mean she'd succeeded in convincing herself it was the best thing to do.

But Cassie's secret hope deflated the moment the Mission House came into view. Scarlett was right out front, packing up a car, and she looked just about ready to head out on the road. Another hour and she would have been gone.

"We lucked out," Adam said, and Cassie nodded.

Scarlett put her hands on her hips and curled her mouth into a smile when they came into view. The look she gave Cassie was sly and peculiar.

"She doesn't seem very surprised to see us," Cassie said. "Or very intimidated."

They climbed out of Adam's car awkwardly. Cassie had the distinct feeling her every gesture was being examined.

"I thought I might be seeing you again," Scarlett said.

"Why is that?" Adam asked.

Scarlett chuckled in a rich, disturbing way. "Just a hunch." She gestured to the house. "Come on inside."

Cassie and Adam followed Scarlett back into the main room. She pictured Scarlett writhing in pain on the floor during their last encounter and could almost hear her begging for mercy.

Adam glanced at the chair he'd been tied to and chose to sit on the couch instead. Cassie remained standing.

"Strange things have been happening to my powers," Scarlett said. "They've been unpredictable. There one minute, gone the next." She made herself comfortable in the chair Adam was avoiding. "Is it happening to you, too?"

"It's because Suzan died," Cassie said. The moment those words left her mouth the truth behind them became real to her in a whole new way.

"Do you remember Suzan?" Adam asked.

Scarlett nodded. "The natural redhead, of course. How'd she die?"

"The hunters killed her," Cassie said.

"Bummer." Scarlett's voice came out without much emotion. "But what does your friend's death have to do with my powers?"

"Our Circle is now incomplete." Adam inched up to the edge of the couch. "And the bind of the Circle means that you're next in line for Suzan's place."

Scarlett had no reaction for a few seconds. "I don't understand. How could it be me?"

"Your mother was Suzan's aunt," Cassie explained. "But nobody knew about her."

The confusion in Scarlett's eyes gradually progressed to surprise, and then delight. "I don't believe it," she said. "And to think I wasted so much time and energy trying to destroy you, Cassie."

Cassie was stone-faced. "I can hardly believe it myself, but here we are."

"And you're willing to initiate me?" Scarlett asked.

"Our friend is dead," Adam said. "And more of us are sure to die if we don't do something. We'll allow you into our Circle because we need your help to defeat the hunters. That's the only reason."

"I'm sorry, what was that?" Scarlett put her hand to her ear. "I couldn't quite hear you. Did you say you *needed* me? That you need my help?"

Adam shot up from the couch. "You know what? Forget this. Cassie, let's go."

Scarlett also stood up and blocked Adam's path to the door. "Relax a little. I'm just playing with you. The fact of the matter is you do need me. But I also need you. We all have something to gain from this."

Scarlett directed her next words at Adam. "Undo that restraining spell, and I'm yours for the taking."

Cassie felt the blood rise to her cheeks and went to Adam's side. "First we set up some ground rules."

Scarlett tossed her hair back and laughed. "You all love your rules, don't you?"

"We don't trust you." Adam's back was rigid and his voice was hard. "And we don't like you. I want that to be clear. One wrong move, and we won't hesitate to do worse than banish you from New Salem. You can bet we'll be watching you."

"Oh, I know you will, honey." Scarlett pouted her dark red lips. "*You* in particular can hardly keep your eyes off me."

Adam flinched and Cassie raised her arm to quiet him. "It's okay," she said. "I expected this."

She stared at Scarlett for a moment with an expression of disgust. A murky voice from the depths of her mind whispered, *Kill her.* But Cassie knew to ignore it, and she also understood that, for Adam's sake, she had to appear confident they were doing the right thing by bringing Scarlett back to New Salem.

"Let's reverse the spell," she said to him. "That's what we came here to do."

Cassie showed no hesitation or doubt as she placed her hand on Scarlett's forehead and began the process of disabling the restraining spell. But deep down inside she was terrified of what she was about to unleash on the Circle, and on her relationship.

As soon as they arrived back in New Salem, Cassie and Adam escorted Scarlett into the dark woods. Cassie steeled herself against the dull throbbing in her gut, the urge to restrain Scarlett again and banish her not only from New Salem but from Adam, the Circle, and her life. But the rest of the group was already gathered, preparing for Scarlett's initiation. There was no turning back now.

Diana was the first to come into view. She was dressed in her white shift and wore the Master diadem upon her head. In her hand was a dagger.

Scarlett stared at the blade of the dagger and at the moonlight shimmering on it. "I see we're not wasting any time," she said. "The situation must really be dire."

"It is," a husky voice behind her said.

Faye was wearing her black ceremonial shift and the leather garter around her leg. She held the silver bracelet out to Cassie. "Put this on," she said.

Cassie was the only leader dressed in her regular

clothes, but they would each wear one of the Master Tools.

Diana squared herself to Scarlett. Her long blond hair hung loose beneath the diadem and reflected the moon in such a way that it cast her face in an ethereal glow. "If you're going to be a member of our Circle," she said, "you have to act like one. This initiation is based on a set of promises."

"You mean rules," Scarlett murmured coolly.

"Yes, rules," Diana replied. "For you and for us to follow."

"Don't even bother trying to talk to her like a human being," Faye said. "She'll never be one of us. Let's just get this over with. Everyone step inside the circle."

Scarlett smiled ingenuously and Cassie led her to her place just outside a gap in the circle that had been drawn into the ground.

Diana stood in the center and formally began the ceremony. She raised the silver dagger to the sky—the same dagger used in Cassie's initiation—and asked, "Who challenges her?"

"I do," Cassie said, at the same time as Faye.

Everyone's eyes bounced back and forth between the two of them. "Faye, I've got this," Cassie whispered, and then much louder, she repeated, "I do. I challenge Scarlett."

Cassie went to the center of the circle and took the silver dagger from Diana. Then she stood before Scarlett with the blade in her outstretched hand. She held it up to Scarlett's throat.

"If there is any fear in your heart," Cassie said, "it would be better for you to throw yourself forward on this dagger than to continue."

Cassie put a little more pressure on the blade, so it pressed lightly into the hollow of Scarlett's neck. "Is there fear in your heart?"

Scarlett smiled. "None."

Cassie stared hard at her, deep into the dark eyes that were just like their father's. It occurred to Cassie that Scarlett's life was completely in her hands. She could slice her open right there like a sheep in a slaughter-house.

"Cassie." Faye sounded faint and far away.

Cassie continued glaring at Scarlett, putting a little more pressure on the blade, just enough to prick the fine surface of Scarlett's skin.

"Cassie!" Diana shouted. "Scarlett gave her answer. Now step away."

Cassie swallowed hard and realized that Faye was at her side, guiding her back to her place on the circle's perimeter. She wrenched the dagger from Cassie's grip and passed it to Diana. Cassie suddenly felt weak.

"Scarlett, please step inside the circle," Diana instructed.

Scarlett did as she was told, and Diana dragged the dagger through the ground to close the circle behind her.

"Now come to the center." Diana raised her arms over Scarlett and asked the initiation questions. "Will you swear to be loyal to the Circle? Never to harm anyone who stands inside it? Will you protect and defend those who do, even if it costs you your life?"

Scarlett smirked before answering. "Yes."

"Will you swear never to reveal the secrets you will learn, except to a proper person, within a properly pre-pared Circle like the one we stand in now? Will you swear to keep these secrets from all outsiders, friends, and ene-mies, even if it costs you your life?"

There was a disturbing triumph in Scarlett's eyes. "Yes," she said.

"By the ocean, by the moon, by your own blood, will you so swear?"

"I will so swear," Scarlett said.

Diana looked over each member of the group. "Scarlett has sworn," she said. "And now I call on the Powers to look at her."

Just as she had when Cassie was initiated, Diana raised the dagger high above her head, with its blade pointed to the sky. She aimed it east, south, west, and north. And then, finally, she pointed it at Scarlett and said:

> *Earth and water, fire and air,*
> *See your daughter standing there.*
> *By dark of moon and light of sun,*
> *As I will, let it be done.*
>
> *By challenge, trial, and sacred vow,*
> *Let her join the Circle now.*
> *Flesh and sinew, blood and bone,*
> *Scarlett now becomes our own.*

And that was it. Just like that, Scarlett was one of them. The Powers had welcomed her and the group had welcomed her, but it was nothing like when Cassie had become a member. There was no hugging, no real sense of welcoming.

Diana and the other members of the Circle did what

they had to do in the best way they knew how, but they didn't have to celebrate it.

"Are we done here?" Scarlett asked disdainfully.

"Yes." Diana sheathed her dagger. "We're done."

Laurel blew out all the candles and collected them, one by one. Cassie was ready to get away from this sham of an initiation as quickly as possible, but Faye pulled her aside.

"Can we talk about what happened back there?" Faye asked.

"Back where?" Cassie asked. "I don't know what you're talking about."

"I think you do." Faye leaned in close to Cassie's ear and brought her voice to a whisper. "The others may be willing to play along and pretend like you didn't almost just make mincemeat of your half sister, but I won't."

"You mean with the dagger?" Cassie said. "I was just testing her. I wanted to scare her."

"Cassie, I saw you. I saw your eyes. We all know what's been happening to you, but everyone's too afraid to talk about it."

"And you expect me to believe that you want to talk about it, why, Faye? Because you're so concerned about my welfare? Or Scarlett's safety?"

"Heck, no. I think you should have stabbed her. It would have made things easier for all of us."

Cassie looked at Faye, stunned, and then Faye cracked a smile. "Okay, maybe that would have been going a little too far."

Cassie let herself laugh for the first time in a while, and Faye looked at her with a strange expression—something like understanding.

"But I'm serious that I think it's a mistake to keep trying to handle all this black magic stuff yourself," Faye said. "It's obviously not working."

Cassie examined Faye's face for a clue as to what she was after. What strategy was she playing? After a moment, Cassie said, "You want me to show you the book."

"Of course I want you to show me the book."

Cassie shook her head. "Nice try." She laughed again.

Suddenly there was a rustling in the woods. Faye turned quickly to locate the source of the sound. They all did.

"We've got a problem." Adam focused on one of the trees in the distance.

CHAPTER 25

From behind a stand of bulky trees came Max, his dad, and the two hunters who'd escaped from the rooftop—Jedediah and Louvera Felton. Each of them held a stone carved into the shape of the hunter symbol—the same relics they'd used to kill Suzan. Scarlett bolted at first sight of the hunters, disappearing into the woods. Why wasn't Cassie surprised? With all her big talk, of course at heart Scarlett was just a coward.

A quick look passed between Diana and Max. He frowned at her with shame and sadness in his eyes, like he might have been there against his will.

"Now!" Mr. Boylan screamed, raising his symbol into the air.

Adam shot his hands toward the principal, calling out a defense spell. Nick tried throwing his energy at him with a fire blast. But Mr. Boylan and all the hunters appeared to be resistant to their magic. They clung to their relics and chanted their own curse, unhindered by anything cast their way.

"We have to get those stones out of their hands," Melanie said.

Together Chris and Doug charged for Louvera's relic, but the moment they came within striking distance, they both dropped to the ground, holding their heads.

Melanie dove for Jedediah's relic, but she was also quick to fall, holding her head as if the relic had struck her.

Cassie, Diana, and Faye were still wearing the Master Tools. They joined hands and moved toward the hunters, chanting, "Earth my body, water my blood, air my breath, and fire my spirit."

Mr. Boylan showed no fear of the Tools. He stepped forward, holding his symbol out to them, muttering the same words Cassie remembered hearing on the rooftop:

I sum eius agens,
I occidere in eius nomen—
I sum eius agens,
I occidere in eius nomen—

Cassie could feel that the Tools weren't working. She felt weak to the bone and powerless, and the bracelet remained cool and lifeless on her arm.

Mr. Boylan seemed to grow stronger every second he continued his chant. He was getting the best of them. Laurel, Deborah, and Sean had all fallen down onto the ground. Cassie could no longer see anyone else. Her own head began to throb, her vision blurred, and she knew it wouldn't be long before she also lost all her remaining strength.

"Cassie," Diana said. "I'm . . ." She folded to her knees.

Max turned to Diana and cried out. He ran to where she'd fallen, standing between her and his father. Mr. Boylan tried to wave him out of the way, but Max wouldn't budge. He placed his stone relic on the ground and raised his arms. "We have to stop this," he said. "Stop the curse."

Tears of joy and relief filled Diana's eyes. Max had come through for her.

Adam appeared at Cassie's side, winded and confused. "What's he doing?" he asked.

The hunters had been thrown off by Max's turnaround. For a brief moment they had ceased chanting, looking to Mr. Boylan for direction, but now they resumed again with full force.

Max's father picked up Max's relic from the ground and held it out for him. "Take this," he said. But Max refused to accept it. He stood tall with Diana behind him.

"Don't make a terrible mistake," his father said. "Obey your destiny."

Max glanced back at Diana and then returned his eyes to his father. "I am obeying my destiny," he said.

The Circle watched Max in awe. There were a few seconds of silence, long enough for Cassie to hear Diana inhale with a quick, shallow breath and stumble to her feet. And then with a swift swipe to the head, Mr. Boylan knocked Max out cold.

Diana dashed to Max's aid, but Jedediah pummeled her with a few ominous words. She spilled onto the ground beside Max's unconscious body.

Laurel crawled over to Cassie, horrified. "Do something," she screamed. "Whatever you did on the roof, do it again."

Faye leaned forward at Cassie's side, breathless. "You have to," she begged. "You're our only hope."

But before Cassie could say a word, Adam winced as if he'd been shot. Then he dropped facedown onto the ground. Faye also buckled and then collapsed, holding her head in her hands.

Cassie looked around. She was the only Circle member still standing. She locked eyes with Mr. Boylan and burned with a feverish heat. Book or no book, she had the power in her, and she knew it. All she had to do was let it take her over.

Cassie centered her mind and took a deep breath. She told herself that just this one time it was okay to give in, to let the darkness wash over her and surge through her veins. But suddenly her legs went out from under her. Her head felt like it had been cracked open, and a splitting pain assured her she'd acted too late. All her energy was being drained from her body. It was the sensation of dying, she was sure of it.

Through her hazy vision, she could see that Max had awakened and was trying to rise to his feet, but the other two hunters were restraining him. They held him back as they continued the curse, their relics still in hand.

The entire Circle had been overpowered. Each of them lay scattered around the muddy ground like insects left for dead. The hunters' chant became louder. Mr. Boylan had closed his eyes and raised his arms to the sky, ecstatic and triumphant. Cassie could hardly believe that after such a long, hard fight it could end so pitifully for her Circle.

But then Mr. Boylan's eyes shot open again and he

suddenly drew back. "Not again," he said. "It can't be possible."

The other hunters anxiously scanned the surrounding area. They'd stopped mumbling their curse and tilted their heads toward the woods to listen.

Cassie faintly heard what they were hearing. Another language, both foreign and familiar. It was Scarlett. She was in the distance, walking toward them, chanting a dark spell.

Jedediah clutched his chest as he had on the roof. His face reddened as he gasped for air, and he screamed for their retreat. He and Louvera backed away from Max and fled in the opposite direction.

Max was dazed. He was squinting his eyes, searching the ground for Diana, clambering like a baby deer new to its hooves. And then he shrieked in pain, clutching his heart.

Chris, Doug, and Sean rose back up to a standing position. Deborah, Laurel, and Melanie did the same. The Circle was regaining its strength even as Max's waned. Diana cried out to Scarlett. "You're killing him!" But Scarlett was unstoppable.

Mr. Boylan hurried to Max and helped him to his feet. "It's an ancient," he said. "We have to run." He steadied Max's arm around his neck.

Max, writhing in agony, allowed his father to drag him away, and within minutes they were gone, swallowed up by the shadowy woods. Tragedy had been averted.

"I guess we showed them," Scarlett said, as she sauntered to the center of the pounded and baffled group. "Or at least I did." Her eyes were still dark from the forbidden spell.

Cassie recognized the aftermath of intense power and pleasure on Scarlett's face. It made Cassie envious, resentful even. How was Scarlett able to tap into her dark magic without losing all control? She appeared able to turn it on and off at will.

"Don't worry," Scarlett said. "I don't expect a thank-you. Not yet anyway." She made her way toward the car. "We'd better get out of here, in case they have any more surprises for us. We need time to regroup and restore our energy."

Everyone, a little dazed, obediently followed behind her as if she'd just proven herself the Circle's most worthy leader.

Cassie, Adam, and Diana hung back.

"I hate to admit it," Diana said. "But if we hadn't initiated her, we'd be dead right now."

"But that was black magic that she used against them."

Adam glanced momentarily at Cassie. "Wasn't it?"

Cassie nodded.

"Well, whatever it was," Diana said, "she did it for us. She had the chance to escape into the woods and leave us for dead, and she didn't."

Adam was in agreement. "We still can't trust her, but maybe she can be useful to us after all."

"Maybe," Cassie said. But she knew better than anyone that one good deed didn't change who someone was.

CHAPTER 26

"You can't hide it from us any longer, Diana," Melanie said. "It was pretty obvious when he risked his life to protect you."

The group was gathered around the coffee table in the secret room trying to figure out what had gone wrong in the woods, when the conversation turned to Diana and Max. But the star-crossed lovers didn't stop some Circle members from nervously eyeing Scarlett, on edge now that she was present for these private conversations.

"He did prove himself out there," Laurel said with a romantic breeziness. "In the moment of truth he chose love."

"Have you two totally lost your minds?" Faye had been seething quietly on the tufted sofa while Melanie and Laurel waxed poetic about Max's turnaround, but she made up for it now by raising the volume of her voice well above theirs. "Max is the enemy. Remember? That's what you all told me. But now that Diana's fallen for him, he's suddenly the second coming?"

"Quit your complaining," Melanie barked back from the opposite side of the coffee table. "You're just jealous. Did you not see what he did for her out there?"

"He did it for all of us," Diana said. "Faye, I know you had feelings for him once. But you have to understand, we really are in love. Can you find it in your heart to be happy for us?"

Faye turned up her nose. "You're going to make me puke," she said, and retreated to her foldout bed.

"Max is dangerous," Chris called out. "You girls need to get the hearts and stars out of your eyes."

"That's right," Doug said. "Love has nothing to do with this. This is war."

Cassie noticed Adam staring down at the wooden floor. Then he glanced at Scarlett, and Cassie caught a brief moment pass between them. Cassie couldn't be sure what it was, but she could tell that regardless of what Adam thought of Max's intentions, he did believe Scarlett had proven herself out in the woods. It was obvious in the humble way he was looking at her. And she returned his gaze with a sly smile.

Cassie's jealousies flared and an image flashed in her mind. This time she saw Scarlett and Adam in bed together—in Cassie's bed—and they were kissing like hungry lovers. The scene was so vivid and graphic it was like Cassie had burst through the door and caught them in real life. Her rage seeped into the vision itself and she willed Scarlett off Adam, then doused her in a blaze of fire. She stepped closer to watch Scarlett's face blacken and melt hauntingly into the flames, and the sight of it brought a wriggling satisfaction to her stomach. She wanted to watch Scarlett perish until there was nothing left of her but ash.

It isn't real. Cassie had to shake herself awake, repeating those words to herself until the image disappeared.

Deborah stood up and stepped to the center of the room. "I think I speak for all, or at least most of us, Diana, when I say we want you to be happy. But apart from that, we're in a bad situation here. Every single one of us is in the crosshairs right now. That's what we need to be focusing on." She paused and Nick picked up where she had left off.

"And, no offense," he said. "But if we get the slightest hint that Max is working against us, we'll take him down. Whether he's your boyfriend or not."

"How do you plan to do that, tough guy?" Scarlett said, finally chiming in. "Since it's clear that the only thing that works against the hunters is dark magic."

She'd been sitting on an ottoman off to the side, alone. The only Circle member willing to be within arm's length of her was Sean, and that was only because she was pretty. But now all eyes turned to her, and she looked to Cassie. "Isn't that right?"

Cassie solemnly nodded. "Yes, that's right. Dark magic is how I forced the hunters to retreat on the roof of the school, and it's what Scarlett used back in the woods."

"But neither of you were able to strip the hunters' relics of their powers," Deborah said. "What we need is a spell that will accomplish that. To remove the threat of the hunters forever. Otherwise they'll just keep coming after us until we're all dead and buried."

Diana winced at Deborah's coldheartedness, but the rest of the group agreed.

"Cassie," Adam said. "Now might be a good time to go get your father's book. Maybe Scarlett can help us with the spell we've been working on."

Cassie's stomach dropped in a freefall.

Scarlett said in a throaty, mocking voice, "That's a great idea, Adam. Why don't you do that, Cassie?"

Cassie looked desperately at Diana, who remained tight-lipped and unmoving. Then she turned back to Adam. "I can't," she said. "I don't have it."

Scarlett rose from her seat. "What do you mean you don't have it?"

"Cassie asked me to keep it safe for her." Diana migrated protectively to Cassie's side. "It's hidden someplace no one will find it."

Faye shot up from where she'd thrown herself down onto her mattress. "Are you kidding me, Cassie? You gave it to Diana and not me?"

"We *all* have a right to see it." Melanie spoke over Faye. "And not just a few pages at a time that Cassie copies for us, but as a whole book. Diana, you should go get it and bring it back here."

"I agree," Laurel said to Cassie. "We're all in this together, we should all know what resources we have."

"None of you understand. It's controlling me!" Cassie screamed.

Everyone fell silent. They all averted their eyes except for Faye, who watched Cassie carefully, and Scarlett, who seemed to be enjoying the show.

"None of you can possibly understand," Cassie repeated. "It's not just the burns. I haven't been myself since I got the book. And if I start using magic from it, I don't know what

I'm capable of doing to the rest of the Circle. Or what using the book could do to all of you."

For a few seconds nobody said anything, and then Diana made an effort to break the quiet. "I'll bring the book back here when Cassie feels she's ready. Not a moment before." She threw an angry glance at Scarlett. "But feel free to whine and moan about it all you want."

There was a sudden *whoosh* at the room's entrance that startled everyone at once. It was the sound of the secret door opening.

Cassie's mom stepped forward and immediately locked eyes with the new face in the room, but her expression wasn't one of unfamiliarity, it was cautious recognition.

"I'm sorry, I didn't mean to interrupt," she faltered.

"That's okay, Mom," Cassie said. "This is Scarlett Forsythe, our newest Circle member."

Her mother's eyes flared. Cassie could tell she had nearly gasped but managed to restrain herself. "Really," she said in a noncommittal tone and forced a smile.

Scarlett grinned at her. "You knew my mother."

Cassie's mom inclined her head slightly and an odd expression crossed her face, like she was trying to determine if this was a nightmare. "Yes. A long time ago. Your resemblance is striking."

"So I've been told." Scarlett spoke loudly, aggressively,

as if she were angry with Cassie's mom simply for being alive when her own mother wasn't.

Cassie positioned herself between them, feeling protective of her mother. "We're okay down here," she said. "Scarlett is one of us now and we're just finishing up some business. You can go up to bed."

Her mother's eyes were still fixed on Scarlett, as if she couldn't bear to look away from her.

Cassie guided her out the door and across the basement, back to the stairs.

"What is she doing here?" her mother hissed.

"We had no choice but to initiate her after Suzan's death. It all happened so fast. We need her and she needs us—at least for now."

"Be careful," her mother whispered, hugging her tight. "You cannot trust her."

"Tell me about it," was all Cassie could bring herself to say.

~~~~~~~~~~~

The Circle decided to crash at Cassie's that night for safety, "to watch over one another," they'd said, but Cassie knew what they'd meant was to watch over Scarlett. Scarlett may have earned her spot in the Circle when she forced the hunters away in the woods, but she was a long way from securing the Circle's confidence. Tonight they would all sleep with one eye open.

Adam had crept into Cassie's bedroom to say good night, and he was taking his time leaving, in no rush to separate from her. He was softly running his fingers up and down the inside of her arm, the way she loved. Cassie didn't want him to leave her either. She wanted him to hold her tight until she drifted to sleep.

Adam leaned in and began kissing her neck, tenderly and quietly. He was being gentle with her, but she could hear the heaviness of his breathing. She understood how much he'd been missing having her this way. But then a knock on the door disturbed them.

"It's Scarlett," the voice on the other side of the door said. "Can we talk?"

Adam held Cassie tighter and shook his head, but Cassie told him it was okay. Reluctantly, he got up and let Scarlett in.

"I'd like to speak to Cassie privately," Scarlett said, dismissing Adam with a flick of her wrist.

"Now?" Adam asked, with a tinge of frustration to his voice.

Scarlett stepped past him and climbed onto Cassie's bed. "Yes, now."

Only after a nod from Cassie did Adam comply. "I'll be right out here on the couch," he said. "If you need anything."

Scarlett smiled at Adam's overprotectiveness and waited for him to close the door before she turned to Cassie and said, "I thought we could tell secrets."

Cassie thought back to their first sleepover, how excited she was to have a sister to share things with. How naive she'd been back then. She wouldn't be fooled again. "Okay," she said icily. "You first."

"I knew you'd say that." Scarlett nudged her on the arm. "I have a secret about . . . dark magic."

Cassie suddenly felt wary, but she reminded herself that her whole Circle was only one scream for help away. "Go on." She braced herself for the worst.

"I can read Black John's book," Scarlett said. "My mom helped teach me before she died."

Scarlett's face was open and serious, and Cassie understood this was no trick. She was telling the truth.

"It's in our blood," Scarlett continued. "The language. You'll have to work to unlock it, but you know how to read the book, too, Cassie."

Cassie called to mind the few words in the book she could comprehend, and it all started to make sense to her. Instinctively, she'd known this all along.

"I understand you're worried about the dark magic taking over," Scarlett said. "But we were built to control it. And with time, you will be able to."

"Why are you telling me all this?" Cassie asked.

Scarlett laughed. "You love to keep those guards up, don't you? I'm telling you all this because we're on the same side now. And I want to defeat the hunters just as much as you do. They've killed people I loved, too."

Cassie thought back to Scarlett explaining how she first came to New Salem on the run from the hunters who had killed her mother—but Cassie doubted that was all there was to it. Then she remembered her daydream from a little while earlier, and how she was able to shake out of her evil thoughts. Maybe Scarlett was right about being able to control the darkness.

"Do you trust me?" Scarlett asked.

Trusting in Scarlett would never come easy. But for right now, Cassie didn't have much of a choice. "No, I don't trust you," she said. "But I do believe you."

"Well, I guess that's a start." Scarlett got up and went to the door. "Get some rest," she said. "We have a big day ahead of us."

She wrapped her hand around the doorknob and then

released it again. "One more thing." She swiveled back around on her heels. "I think it's adorable that you and Adam are trying so hard to stick together through all this. I am so impressed by how accepting you've been." She paused to draw the moment out, relishing it. "About the cord between him and me, I mean. You must have taken lessons from your friend Diana."

Cassie felt something inside her tighten and then unhinge. A caustic taste like battery acid filled her mouth, tainting her voice with venom. "You stay away from Adam."

"I just complimented you, Cassie. Don't go spoiling it with your awful temper." Scarlett lifted her eyebrows and pursed her full lips. And with that, she was gone.

CHAPTER 27

"What did Scarlett say to you last night?" Adam asked. He and Cassie were taking an early morning walk out on the bluff before the others woke up.

"A lot." Cassie stared off at the horizon as she spoke, imagining herself getting lost somewhere in that line between the ocean and the sky. She didn't have the heart to tell Adam that Scarlett knew about the cord between them.

"She got me thinking about my power," Cassie said. "I don't want to live in fear anymore. In fear of myself and what I'm capable of."

"You shouldn't have to." Adam was trying to be supportive, even though Cassie's dark powers were far beyond his realm of understanding. He was afraid for her and she knew it. In his eyes she could see how much he wished he could take on the burden himself.

"So what does Scarlett suggest you do?" Adam asked.

"She said if I embrace my dark magic I can learn to control it. Which has obviously been my problem lately. Controlling it."

Adam stepped around Cassie to face her, blocking her view over the bluff. "Do you think you can learn to do that?"

"I don't know what I think. I'm not sure if I can even trust my own thoughts."

Adam wrapped his arms around Cassie and pulled her in. She could smell the salt water drifting in the air and off his skin. "Well, I'll tell you what I think. I think we won't know until you try. And I will stand by you every step of the way, no matter what."

"But what if it goes badly? What if it changes me, more than it already has?"

"None of us knows what the future holds or who we'll become, Cassie. But I do know that we can be true to who we are right now. And that applies to me loving you, and you loving me, and to you being able to connect to the light inside of you. That's not going anywhere."

Adam kissed the top of Cassie's head and then let her go. "But you also have to trust yourself. You have to have faith in your own fundamental goodness."

Cassie nodded. "I think I'm ready to."

Without another word, Adam swooped in and kissed her. She almost laughed—it was the last thing she expected him to do at that moment. She had been on the verge of asking him about the brief look he had exchanged with Scarlett the night before, the one that had set her off in an internal jealous rage.

But as she leaned in to kiss him back, she forgot all about that. She could feel the sun on her back and hear the ocean in the distance. Sometimes Adam knew just what to do to make everything all right.

———

Everyone was groggy from sleep and clinging to coffee mugs when Cassie announced a Circle meeting in the secret room. Faye sat with her bedspread still wrapped around her and even Diana looked like she could have used another hour of rest, but Cassie's news was sure to wake them right up.

"I've done some thinking since yesterday," she said to the group as they gathered round. "And I've decided that Diana should bring my father's book here for Scarlett to take a look at."

Scarlett met Cassie's eyes and something passed between them, a beat of understanding. But Cassie quickly looked away, breaking the moment. She didn't want to feel like she had too much in common with her sister.

"I know the spell my father used will work to defeat the hunters." Cassie had everyone's full attention now. "And Scarlett can translate it for us. She understands the book's language."

All attention spun to Scarlett's direction. Faye tossed her blanket off like a cape.

Diana's mouth dropped open. "Scarlett can translate it for us?" she repeated. Her green eyes flashed at Cassie. "That's a huge responsibility for Scarlett to take on alone."

Faye smirked. "What Diana means is, how do we know we can trust her? If none of us know the difference. She can tell us to do anything she wants."

"Because I'm trusting her," Cassie said.

"That's it?" Faye was expecting more.

Cassie's heart thumped and thrashed within her chest, but she maintained her strength and composure. "And because it's time to end this, once and for all. Scarlett has no reason to mislead us. She wants to be rid of the hunters just as much as we do."

"Hear, hear," Nick said from his sleeping bag. "So when and where do we go after them?"

"I can help with that." Diana shook off the surprise of the prior moment and spoke up. "Max knows where the hunters assemble. I bet we can infiltrate one of their meetings."

"We can ambush them," Nick said. "When they least expect it."

"But in exchange," Diana deferred to Cassie, "I ask that the Circle spare Max from whatever the curse will do."

"No way," Faye shouted. "There's no reason to believe Max's puppy-dog love for Diana is any more real than his feelings for me were."

"Faye, we've been through this already," Melanie said. "You have to let it go."

"I'm not going to let it go," Faye insisted. "Because it was the same thing—"

"It wasn't the same thing." Diana's cheeks were flushed and her eyes were sharp. "It wasn't even close to the same thing. I've tried to be nice about this, Faye, but you're making that impossible. Do you need me to break it down for you? *You* were using magic to mess with Max's mind. *I* have found my soul mate. Do you get the difference?"

Faye defied Diana with a fixed stare. "As a leader of this Circle I hereby raise the issue of Diana's inability to be impartial when considering Max's trustworthiness."

"Oh shut up, Faye," Melanie said.

"Melanie!" Cassie shouted. "You're out of line. Faye has the floor and she's raised a legitimate issue to the Circle."

Diana swung around to look at Cassie. "Seriously? You're going to let her go with this?"

"She has a right to voice her concern," Cassie said apologetically.

"Thank you, Cassie." Faye stood up to better command the space. She eyed Diana, Melanie, and Laurel, who were clustered on top of Laurel's bed. Then she turned to Chris, Doug, and Deborah scattered around Nick's sleeping bag on the floor. And finally she rested her eyes on Scarlett, who was seated off to the side with only Sean nearby.

"I know what you all saw in the woods," Faye said. "I was there. I know Max stood up to his father to protect Diana. But I also saw Max leave with his father, as you all did. Not with us. With him."

Faye paused to glare specifically at Melanie before continuing. "Yet now we're going to trust Max to tell us where to find the hunters, where to find his father, so we can attack them on their own turf. Do I have to be the one to say it? Am I the only one who thinks this sounds like a trap?"

Melanie was quiet. They all were. Even Cassie had to admit Faye had a valid argument.

"Faye?" Diana said. "You're right." She took control of the floor. "I am partial. I do believe Max will truthfully lead us to the hunters, and in good faith I believe he should be spared from whatever negative effects the curse will have. But the rest of you are free to decide for yourselves."

Diana turned to Cassie. "I propose a vote to declare the Circle's decision, and I will abstain from that vote."

After a few more seconds of tense quiet, Cassie called on Melanie. "Will you do the honors, please?"

Melanie rose, cleared her throat, and said in her cool, authoritative tone: "All in favor of sparing Max if he leads us to the hunters, raise your hands."

To Cassie's surprise, enough hands shot immediately up to decide the vote without counting. Even at a time like this there still seemed to be an inclination among the group to align themselves with Diana.

Melanie beamed with satisfaction. "The majority of the Circle believes Max can be trusted. And we promise to spare him."

"Thank you," Diana said. Cassie wasn't sure she'd ever seen Diana more sincere, and that was saying something.

Faye shook her head and sneered at her. "Cry your tears of joy now. But if Max betrays us, neither of you will be spared. I'll see to that myself."

Cassie parted her lips to speak but instead found herself looking at Faye, whose eyes reflected a concentrated power. Then she quickly turned her attention to Diana and said, "I'm sure it won't come to that."

But Cassie wasn't really sure. Maybe Diana was being naive. Maybe she was, too.

Scarlett whispered something into Adam's ear and he nodded. It was getting more and more difficult to determine who was trustworthy anymore.

CHAPTER 28

Scarlett sat at Cassie's desk, poring over Black John's Book of Shadows while Cassie and Adam worked on their laptops—but Cassie was really keeping an eye on Scarlett. She watched Scarlett's eyes scan the book's text line by line, occasionally jotting down notes on her memo pad. Some of the time Scarlett just paged through the book, fully absorbed and too excited by what she was reading to slow down enough to copy it down. She was supposed to be looking specifically for the witch-hunter curse, but Cassie could see she kept getting sidetracked.

"Knock knock," Diana said, as she stepped inside. "How's the research coming?"

"Slowly." Adam shut his laptop.

"Well, I have some news that might cheer you up." Diana sat down on Cassie's bed. "I just talked to Max. He told me the witch hunters have their headquarters set up in the caves on the beach."

But Diana's news was overshadowed by Scarlett's shout of excitement.

"I found it!" Scarlett said. She stood up so fast her chair fell backward onto the floor. "This is it. The spell Black John used against the hunters."

Cassie, Adam, and Diana all rushed to the book to see it for themselves, forgetting everything that came before.

The page Scarlett held open looked much like the rest of the book. It was composed of a few short lines—inky black squiggles and glyphs.

"Are you sure this is the one?" Cassie asked.

"I'm positive." Scarlett ran her fingers over the page, scanning its contents again. "And it's not even that complicated. It'll be easy for the Circle to memorize."

"Are you sure? Any small mistake, and who knows what we could do to them, or even to ourselves," Diana said.

"You'll see," Scarlett said to Diana in a patronizing tone. "It'll be as simple as singing a song in a language you don't understand. All you have to do is hit the tones right. The deeper meaning is beside the point."

"How does the curse work?" Diana asked, staring down at the book's illegible text. "What will it do to the hunters?"

Scarlett grinned. "Don't worry. It'll happen so fast they'll hardly feel a thing."

"But what exactly will it do to them?" Diana persisted.

"It'll take away the power from their stone relics," Scarlett said. "And break the bond between the hunters and their marks."

"So we'll all be unmarked." Cassie looked the spell over with Adam. Based on her instincts and their limited research, everything Scarlett said seemed right.

"And anyway, Diana," Scarlett added, "Max is being spared. As long as he's nowhere near his relic when we cast this, he'll be fine. So what are you so nervous about?"

Cassie let the comment pass. "All right then," she said. "We're just about ready to do this."

Adam turned to Diana. "Those caves where the hunters have their headquarters are down by the rockier shores. We'll need rowboats to get to them."

Diana pulled out her phone. "Max can help with

that. If it's all right with you, Cassie, I think he should be included in this discussion."

Cassie hesitated, but Adam didn't. "Are you planning to invite him over? Here?"

Diana squared herself to Adam. "Max is turning his back on hundreds of years of his own ancestry and is probably going to be disowned by his father for helping us. So yes, I'm planning to invite him over so he's clear on how all this will go down."

Adam took a breath that sounded like assent and Cassie told Diana to go ahead. Within the hour Max was standing in her bedroom with his muscular arms crossed over his chest, hovering over her father's book.

Scarlett showed him the spell and he squinted at it. He scratched the stubble on the side of his face and looked at Diana. "Can you ensure their safety?"

"The spell will deactivate the relics," Scarlett said. "That's what it's designed to do. Beyond that, none of us are in a position to ensure anything. This is a battle we're going into, after all. War doesn't come with guarantees for either side."

Max chewed on his thick lower lip, mulling things over in his mind. "Well, I want to be there to make sure both sides play fair." He rested his sharp eyes on Scarlett, understanding somehow that it was her spearheading this crusade. "Consider me the referee."

Scarlett grinned. "Then I guess the only question left is, how soon can we leave?"

They all looked to Max for the answer.

"Tonight," he said confidently, reaching for Diana's hand. "We'll go tonight. The sooner we get this over with, the better."

They had an hour till dusk, just the right amount of time to arrive at the caves in sunlight, and to depart shrouded beneath the cover of night. It took three boats to get them all there. Cassie, Adam, Diana, and Scarlett were at the front, under Max's guidance. As he rowed them closer and closer to the caves, Cassie's nerves started to get the best of her, and she suddenly wished they'd composed a backup plan. She hadn't wanted to appear doubtful at the time, but now that they were sitting out in the water with only Max's word to go on, Cassie wished the Circle had at least considered an escape strategy. What if Max was simply delivering them to the hunters' lair like cargo?

Cassie looked to Faye in the boat behind theirs. They locked eyes and Cassie immediately understood that Faye was ready for anything. She was perched on the edge of her boat's bow, watching and calculating. Cassie gave her a nod. For once, Faye's suspicious, cunning nature served as the most necessary comfort, and Cassie was thankful for it. If this turned out to be a trap, Faye was fully prepared to take Max out to save the Circle—and Cassie would join her.

As their boats neared the caves, the hulking fissures grew larger but no less threatening. By the time they had drifted within walking distance of the main cave's entrance, Cassie got the sense that she was about to step into the mouth of a stone dragon.

"We're here," Max said somberly. "Get up slowly unless you feel like going for a swim."

He smiled then and Cassie recognized the warmth in his face for the first time. She returned his expression as affectionately as she could. In a way, Max's predicament wasn't so different from her own. Like Cassie, he was caught between two opposing sides, between dark and light, his father's nature and his own free will. It couldn't have been a simple decision for him to assist them.

"Thank you," Cassie said to him, hoping to relay some sentiment of camaraderie.

Max nodded, and Cassie said a silent prayer that they were right to rely on him. For his sake and hers.

Cassie climbed out of her rowboat carefully and reached for Adam to steady her on solid ground. She squeezed his hand tightly, needing him close to her now more than ever. It occurred to Cassie that if this attack went poorly, if they failed, it could mean their deaths. These moments could very well be their last. Then a far scarier thought crossed Cassie's mind. What if she survived but Adam didn't? The idea of going on without him was unfathomable to her.

Cassie tried to absorb every detail of Adam as he was now. His electric-blue eyes and wild hair, and the strength that shone in his features even at the worst of times—perhaps especially at the worst of times.

"I don't want to let go of your hand," Cassie said.

"That's good, because I won't let you." Adam brought her fingers to his lips. "Ever."

The whole Circle joined hands then, to link their power. They walked toward the caves in a long line, ready to recite the dark chant they'd memorized.

Cassie's stomach twisted with fear and she struggled with the urge to return to the boats and row home. She glanced back to watch Max heading toward the caves behind them. He would be watching the confrontation from a safe distance. The look on his face was one of love and honor and he was focused solely on Diana. Any residual anxiety Cassie had that Max was leading them into a trap fell away. The cord that connected Max to Diana connected him to the entire Circle—and he was as devoted to this mission as the rest of them.

Candlelight was the first thing Cassie noticed upon entering the cave. It flickered in orange and yellow flashes against the wall, illuminating their way deeper into the bowels of the dark cavern.

Cassie could hear the hunters' soft mumbling before she could see them. There they were: Mr. Boylan, Jedediah Felton, and Louvera Felton, along with two others Cassie hadn't seen before. They were gathered just where Max said they'd be and they were kneeling in a meditative state, performing some kind of ritual. They all had their eyes closed and their heads bowed toward an intricately composed altar. Their ancient relics lay on the ground beside them.

Adam gripped Cassie's hand tighter, and with her other hand Cassie squeezed Diana's fingers in her own. She was suddenly acutely aware of her own breath and the slight sound her own footsteps made upon the gravelly cave floor. She got the distinct feeling that the spell they were about to perform filled her heart and lungs. It rushed through her veins.

This is it, she thought, and she could hardly contain her urgent desire to begin spewing forth the words. They contained her every wish, hope, fear, and need.

The hunters remained motionless, clueless to their impending invasion. It was perfect timing. The words, or sounds really, that Cassie had memorized formed on her lips almost of their own accord. They had fully taken her over. The same must have been true for all the Circle members. Each of them appeared entranced, melded to the spell just as Cassie was.

The twelve of them continued forward, all-powerful and bathed in darkness. They cast the curse, chanting in unison, before the hunters had any idea they'd even arrived.

CHAPTER 29

It felt different from any magic Cassie had ever done before. The energy behind the words surged through her like it did when she had uttered the spell on the rooftop, but this was exponentially more powerful. It had the strength of the whole Circle behind it. The cave started to tremble and shake around them. Rocks crumbled to the ground. The elements seemed to be bending to the Circle's will.

The hunters woke from their trance in a panic. Cassie registered the terror in each of their faces and the pure shock of being ambushed in their safe space. They'd been caught with their every defense down.

The hunters began reciting the same words from the

rooftop and the woods, and their relics brought out the marks on each member of the Circle. Like on the rooftop before Suzan was killed, the hunter symbols glowed brightly upon each of their chests. But against the Circle's curse, the hunters' relics had no other effect. Mr. Boylan shook his like a remote control with a faulty battery, frustrated and enraged by its failure to perform.

Out of desperation, he picked up a rock from the ground and threw it at Cassie. The other hunters followed his lead, grabbing for whatever they could throw. But the Circle remained untouched. The air around them deflected the rocks and foreign objects hurled their way like a protective force field. The Circle's command was impenetrable.

Cassie felt calm and more in control of her magic than ever. And never before had all the members of the Circle worked together so seamlessly, so machinelike in their efficiency. Maybe Cassie had underestimated them, and herself.

The hunters quickly weakened beneath the effects of the spell. Scarlett said it would be quick and painless, that it would be over before the hunters knew what hit them. It was hitting them now with full force. Mr. Boylan swayed back and forth on two wobbly legs, no longer able to even raise his arms in defense. The skin on his face and neck turned ashen and withered. He seemed to age decades right before Cassie's eyes.

The old man hunter, Jedediah, dropped to his knees, holding his head in his hands. He twisted his white hair around his wrinkled fingers and opened his mouth to scream, but no sound escaped. The sight of him reminded Cassie of a famous painting—that ghostly face wide-mouthed with shock. Like the painting itself, the old man's shriek was still and silent.

Louvera, his daughter, lifted up her stone relic like a shield and waved it back and forth in an attempt to protect herself. But her hands shook so furiously she could barely hold on to it. It slipped from her grip and hit the ground with a thud. She crawled around on all fours, urgently trying to recover it.

The spell was working without a flaw. Cassie noticed that the hunter mark on her chest had begun to fade. With every second, the symbol grew dimmer, weaker, as if losing its charge. It couldn't be long now before the relics were drained of all their power and their marks were erased for good. Then the Circle would be safe, and the hunters would never be a threat to them again.

A strange calm and optimism came over Cassie. Her

mind drifted to a kinder place, where she imagined a future for herself and her friends free from this heavy ancient rivalry. They were so close now to turning their world into one where Diana and Max would be allowed to love each other and none of them would have to hide in secret rooms or caves. Hunter and witch alike, they would all be released.

Then Jedediah fell backward from his knees, flat onto his back. His ice-blue eyes were open and unblinking, but they were sapped of all emotion, all feeling. Cassie remembered that same cold look in others she had once known and loved—her grandmother, Melanie's aunt Constance, and Suzan. She knew the look well, and she immediately understood that it wasn't just the old man's powers that had been taken away—it was his life.

Louvera tried desperately to crawl to him, but she couldn't make it. A moment later, she went limp with the same lifeless cold hardened to her eyes.

"No!" Max rushed in from just outside the cave's entrance. "You're killing them!" he screamed.

But Cassie couldn't stop. None of them could. The spell had been unleashed and it was working through the Circle now. The words came from their own lips, but they were merely spectators to their effect.

"You have to stop!" Max shouted directly into Diana's face, but she made no reaction. It was as if her eyes couldn't even see him.

Passive as empty vessels, the Circle brought the other two hunters down to the ground, dead. Max just stood there, horrified. He could do nothing as his fellow hunters fell like dominoes all around him. Without his relic, he was both immune to the curse and powerless in trying to stop it.

He ran to his father, wrapped his arms around him, and tried to lift him up. "Let's get you out of here," he said.

His father appeared unsure if it was really his son who'd come to his aid, or if it was just a mirage. Either way, he was too feeble to be moved.

Max started to cry. "Dad, I'm so sorry," he said. "Forgive me, please."

Mr. Boylan made no response. He could only gaze up at his boy, bewildered and terrified.

"I love you," Max said. "Can you hear me, Dad? I love you."

But his father's eyes had turned to stone. His breath had ceased. It was only his lifeless body lying in Max's arms.

The spell ended itself at the moment of his death.

Everyone in the Circle suddenly woke up, as if from a dream, and looked at one another, stunned. There was a slight edge of relief in the air. They'd won; they understood that much. But had they just . . . killed?

Cassie glanced at Adam. He looked pale and sick, like he might faint.

Diana seemed a little dazed, too, unable to figure out what had just occurred.

Cassie spoke up for her. "Max," she said. "We had no idea that was going to happen. The spell was only supposed to disable the relics. We would have never performed it if we knew the hunters would lose their lives. That's not how our Circle does things."

"You just killed my father," Max said. "He's dead! Do you understand that?" He passed his eyes despicably over each member of the Circle. "I trusted you," he said. "And you betrayed me." He set his father's body gently down and stepped back with tears streaming down his face.

He glared at Diana. "Don't follow me," he said, and the way he said it sounded like a brutal threat. Then he ran from the cave and quickly disappeared from their sight.

Diana appeared stunned, but Cassie could feel her best friend's heartbreak as her own. The guilt and remorse she must have been suffering was unimaginable, enough to put her into a state of shock.

Cassie stepped slowly toward her. She placed her hand upon Diana's shoulder, hoping to offer her some comfort. But Diana focused sharply on Cassie in a way that brought her to a frightened halt. Diana's eyes were black as marbles.

"He may flee thither," she said. "But he shall be slain before his enemies." Her voice was gravelly and harsh, nothing like its regular tone.

Cassie was too alarmed to move a muscle. "Diana?" she asked. "Are you—"

"Let us rejoice in our victory." Diana turned grandly to Scarlett. "Thine, O leader," she said, bowing to Scarlett, "is the greatest power. And thou art exalted as head above all."

Scarlett nodded and Cassie noticed the corners of her mouth raise up ever so slightly. "I told you I'd get my Circle," she said.

CHAPTER 30

Cassie looked around in confusion. Something strange was happening to all the members of the Circle.

Adam was sneering oddly. His hands were balled into fists and he was grinding his teeth. There was sweat dripping from his forehead down the front of his face, but he seemed not to notice. He also stared at Cassie with narrowed blackened eyes.

A shiver ran down Cassie's spine. "Scarlett," she said. "Tell me what you've done to them."

"I didn't do anything." Scarlett smirked. "They did it to themselves, casting that spell against the hunters. Any spell cast from our family's book by a nonfamily member calls on our bloodline. It gave the perfect portal into our world for a few unsettled spirits."

Cassie looked around at her friends, now all strangers to her. Sean was mumbling in an incoherent language while Chris laughed like a lunatic and Doug convulsed in a fit on the ground. Melanie's and Laurel's faces had altered. They looked nothing like themselves, and they chattered in voices that weren't their own—Melanie's was deep and husky while Laurel's was high-pitched and playful like a child's.

"I am falsely accused," Melanie declared, while rocking forward and back.

Laurel laughed and clapped, and replied in a piercing singsong, "But you will be condemned to hang."

"Meet the family," Scarlett said.

Cassie wavered. "I don't understand."

"Some of them are still working their way through." Scarlett gestured toward Chris, Doug, and Sean. "But they'll be up and talking like the others soon."

"Who are they?"

Scarlett smiled. "Our ancestors. These are the people who passed down Black John's Book of Shadows."

Cassie looked around at her friends, the truth registering slowly: speaking in tongues, convulsions, changes in vocal intonation and facial expression, superhuman strength.

"The Circle is possessed," she said.

Scarlett rolled her eyes. "Well, duh. These spirits have been waiting to manifest for hundreds of years, to get their power back. And we gave it to them."

Adam stepped forward. His hands were no longer balled into fists and he'd stopped sweating, but his eyes remained dead and black. His body must have been fighting the possession before, but it had now been fully overcome.

He nodded confidently at Cassie and then bowed before Scarlett. "In shackles no more," he said. "To you I am indebted." He lifted her hand to his lips and kissed it.

"Oh yeah," Scarlett said, grinning. "And I'm their leader."

"You're not my leader," Faye called out. She blinked her eyes and looked around, surveying the situation. She appeared a little dazed, but her eyes had returned to their normal color.

Cassie exhaled with relief. "Faye, thank goodness you're all right."

Faye tossed back her mane of black hair and tilted her head. Just as quickly as Faye had seemed normal, her eyes went dark as night. Cassie started backing away in fear. Scratches and bite marks were reddening upon Faye's hands and arms, and eel-like lesions were forming on her neck and face.

"I'm on your side, Cassie," Faye said, moving closer still. "And I want you to be on my side."

"Cassandra holds the book. She is ours," a bold voice behind Cassie said. It was Adam. His features were now firm and serious.

Diana curled her fingers and twitched. "Cassandra shall not be against us; her blood is required."

Cassie continued her backward retreat from the group and realized Scarlett had disappeared. She caught sight of her just as she was about to flee through the mouth of the cave.

"So this was your plan all along?" Cassie ran after Scarlett, shouting. "To poison us this way just so you could have a black magic Circle?"

Scarlett whipped around and put her hands on her hips. "What was it you asked me back at the Mission House? 'Who's Daddy's favorite?' Now you have your answer."

"But none of us have to be this way."

Scarlett continued toward the water and showed no sign of slowing down or even listening.

"Bring us the book, dear one," Adam called out.

"I was falsely accused, but the book shall set us free," Melanie's deep voice repeated.

Of course. Scarlett was going home to get their father's Book of Shadows. But there was no way Cassie was going to let that happen. The dark energy was still coursing through her as well—the remnants of the evil spell remained in her veins. She reached for it mentally, through her own blood and bones. She raised her hands and harnessed every trace of its power toward Scarlett and shouted out, "*Non fugam!*"

Scarlett was instantly thrown backward, as if she'd run up against a pane of glass.

From the ground, she turned to Cassie, stunned. "You didn't."

"*Congelasco,*" Cassie said, freezing Scarlett in place.

Then without hesitation, Cassie lifted her hands to the sky. "*Spelunca est a carcere!*"

Now no one but Cassie was free to leave the cave. Squeals came from the entire Circle as they scrambled in vain to follow her.

"She doth betray us!" Diana shouted.

"Cassandra," Adam nobly called to her. "You're making a terrible mistake."

But before any of them had the chance to try to stop her, Cassie ran for the water's edge. She climbed into one of the boats and set the oars with a splash. She rowed hard, still facing the mouth of the cave. The sun was setting in vivid pinks and purples, outlining the cave's arching shape in a brilliant silhouette. Under any other circumstances, Cassie would have considered the sight of it beautiful.

CHAPTER 31

Cassie arrived back at her house in a cold sweat. Her clothes had been splashed wet from her furious rowing; she'd wanted to get as far away from the caves as fast as she could. Now she was safe in her bedroom, but she was alone—she'd never been so alone in her entire life. Her friends and her one true love were lost to her. Her mother was out, but even if she were home, how could Cassie explain this terrible series of events, especially when it began with her disobeying her mother's warning? This was all her fault. And only she could fix it. It was just Cassie, now, and her book.

She turned to where it was resting on her desk among

loose pens and paper clips, misleadingly tranquil. Because it was only posing as a book. It wasn't just a bunch of pages sewn together within a cover—it was an entity, alive as she was. Cassie understood that now. She took the book into her hands and sat with it on the edge of her bed, holding it in her lap.

She remembered the last time she had sat like this, in this same position, when her mother first presented her with it. Cassie had made so many mistakes since then.

Cassie ran her fingers over the book's aged, leather binding. When her mother first offered it to her she'd told Cassie that in the wrong hands, it could be extremely dangerous. But what she hadn't known then was that even in the right hands it was extremely dangerous. Her mother had assured her that she was strong enough to handle it, but she wasn't. Cassie wasn't nearly strong enough then.

She was now.

Cassie traced the embossment of the book's cover symbol with the tip of her pointer finger. She dug her fingernails into the indentations already scratched into its surface. The book still felt cruel in her hands, but this time would be different. This time she knew exactly what she was in for, and she would do it right.

She took a deep breath and cracked the book open again, as if for the first time.

Her eyes immediately melded to the page, to the words scrawled upon the paper's yellowed surface. At first they appeared much the same as before, but then the text began to slowly wilt and lose its color. The squiggly lines and archaic symbols seemed to lighten and float up from the page. They reshaped and rearranged themselves into new forms, and the curl of each brushstroke straightened along a level plane of letters Cassie recognized. Suddenly she could decipher the book's language and translate it at once to simple English.

Specific words jumped out at her: *spiritus immundus*, evil spirit; *daimonion*, demon.

Nytramancia, the black art.

Some of the words formed into what Cassie understood were titles of other books. *Das puch aller verpoten kunst, ungelaubens und der zaubrey*. The Book of All Forbidden Arts, Heresy and Sorcery. *De Exorcismis et Supplicationibus Quibusdam*. Of Exorcisms and Certain Supplications.

Sacrifices, Pacts.

Conjurations, Commanding Spirits.

These were the dark rites Cassie would have to learn in order to save her friends—and Adam. She must master the book's evil, not be afraid of it, and not be ashamed of her connection to it. It was her destiny—there was no question. But she didn't know how she was going to do it alone.

COMING SOON

Created by the #1 *New York Times* bestselling author

L. J. SMITH

Written by Aubrey Clark

THE SECRET CIRCLE

the Temptation